THE DADDY AND THE DOM

Mafia Ménage Trilogy #2

JULIA SYKES

Copyright © 2021 by Julia Sykes

All rights reserved.

No part of this book may be reproduced in any form or by any electronic or mechanical means, including information storage and retrieval systems, without written permission from the author, except for the use of brief quotations in a book review.

Cover image: Wander Aguiar Photography

Cover design: Popkitty Design

Chapter One
ASHLYN

My frozen skin was icier than the cold tiles at my back, a searing contrast to the heated blood that pounded a head-splitting drumbeat in my ears. My racing heart slammed against my ribcage, inflicting a bruising ache deep in my chest.

The wicked scar carved into my attacker's face twisted on a leer, and his hot breath burned my frozen cheeks. His wiry body pressed into mine, the sharp edges of his joints pinning me in place. Something hard jammed into my side: the gun he'd used to threaten me and compel my silence.

All my muscles locked up with the sudden, primal knowledge of mortal danger. One wrong move, and a bullet would tear through my stomach.

He leaned in close, his rough stubble scraping my cheek.

"You're very pretty." His oily words oozed over my neck, leaving a toxic trail. "I can see why Joseph likes you. I'm sure he'd be heartbroken if anything happened to you."

Sticky warmth painted my skin, and when he pulled away, his face was a gory mess. Blood spilled over his thin lips, cut raw by his broken, jagged teeth.

Joseph had done that. He'd smashed the man's jaw when he'd come to my defense.

Horror was a lead weight in my stomach, and I managed to tear my eyes from the nauseating sight of his ruined face. Frantically, I searched the cramped bathroom for my savior, the man I loved.

But Joseph wasn't there. I was alone with this monstrous man, completely powerless to escape him.

"You're very pretty," he said again, his tone roughed with sick hunger. "Maybe I'll pass you around to my friends until they get bored, and then I'll kill you."

Shadows thickened in the corners of the small space, growing into dark, indistinct silhouettes of towering men.

A second hard length pressed into my hip, larger than the gun shoved into my side.

I thrashed like a trapped animal, and my shriek

echoed through the bathroom, rebounding against the tiles to pierce my eardrums. The shadows closed in on me, trailing frozen fingers over my flesh.

My wordless scream coalesced into Joseph's name, begging for him to save me...

"Ashlyn! Wake up, angel." The strong fingers that closed around my shoulders were warm and calloused; nothing like the icy, grasping claws of my shadowy attackers.

My eyes snapped open, and I finally found the intense, flame-blue stare of my savior.

"Joseph!" I half-sobbed his name and buried my face against his chest, breathing in his comforting, masculine scent.

His steady heat sank into my frigid flesh, but the shadows still clung to my mind with icy, dark tendrils. I pressed closer to him, struggling to fully surface from the nightmare and ground myself in the safety of his strong arms.

I barely had time to register two of Joseph's thundering heartbeats beneath my ear before a deafening *bang* tore through the room. The feel of my attacker's gun was a phantom pain rammed into my side. The terror that'd barely begun to ebb away surged again, and I cried out as my nightmare eclipsed reality.

"Jesus, Marco!" Joseph snapped. He pulled me tighter to his chest, and the pressure of his muscular arms around my shaking body reassured me of his protective presence. "It's okay, angel," he murmured, pressing a tender kiss to my forehead. "You're safe."

"I heard screaming." The rough growl should've made my insides quake, but I recognized Marco's rumbling voice.

My face lifted from Joseph's chest, my eyes searching for my other fierce savior. I hadn't longed for Marco in my dream, but now that his powerful aura pulsed into the room, I was desperate to catch sight of him. I wanted to reassure myself that he was real, too. That both of these immensely strong men were here to shelter me, like they'd promised.

My eyes found Marco, and my breath caught in my throat. His ripped, muscular body was impossibly broader and more intimidating than I'd ever realized. His sculpted chest was bare, and his defined abs bunched tight with coiled aggression. He wore nothing but a pair of black sweatpants slung low on his hips. His massive physique was on full, hulking display.

The sight of his towering frame swelling to fill the doorway should've been scary as hell, but I released a shuddering sigh as relief rolled through me.

"It was just a nightmare." Joseph addressed Marco in clipped tones, and he pulled me closer to his hard body.

The cold light that glittered over Marco's obsidian eyes melted, and the ferocious snarl eased from his rough-hewn features. "You had a nightmare, princess?"

He took a step toward me, and my surroundings finally solidified. I was in Marco's bedroom, where I'd been sleeping with Joseph.

At some point after he'd whisked me away from the dangerous encounter at the restaurant, Marco had carried me up here and tucked me beneath the plush duvet, ensuring I was warm after my bone-chilling confrontation with their enemy. I barely remembered falling asleep in Joseph's arms, exhausted and shaky from the frightening experience. The trauma of being cornered and threatened by a mobster must've followed me down into sleep, triggering my night terror.

Marco took another step toward me, moving with slow, easy grace that was entirely at odds with the pure menace that'd rolled off him in waves only seconds ago. He'd stormed in here and rushed to my defense after hearing me scream.

I noticed the dent in the wall behind him, where he'd flung open the door with enough force that the brass handle had damaged the plaster. All that strength, all that ferocity…

For me. He'd come running to protect me the moment he'd thought I was in danger.

My stomach did a funny flip, and a small shiver raced over my skin. I wasn't scared of Marco. Not at all. But this display of his brute strength and intense protectiveness made me quake for darker, more feminine reasons.

Joseph misinterpreted my trembling and rubbed his hands over my pebbled flesh. My cheeks burned as I realized I was ogling Marco while clinging to Joseph. I tucked my face closer to his chest, hiding my confusing response to his best friend's powerful presence.

"I've got this, Marco." Joseph's warning words rumbled through the room.

Marco's low grunt snagged my attention, and my eyes were immediately drawn to him once again. He'd stopped dead in his tracks, still as a granite statue. His jaw ticked, and his black eyes raked over my trembling body before returning to my face. He studied me with that unwavering, penetrating stare for several unnerving seconds.

His fists flexed at his sides just once before he gave Joseph a curt nod and turned on his heel.

"Wait!" I called out, the plea bursting from my aching chest before I could think better of it. Less than a minute ago, Marco had been all softness and concern when he'd asked about my nightmare. Now, he was stiff and cold again. Aloof after Joseph's sharp dismissal.

Joseph thought he was sheltering me from further distress, but Marco was the one who was upset.

Something tugged at my heart when his hulking body jerked to a halt, and he turned back to face me. His dark brows were drawn low over his eyes, the glower shielding him from me.

But that glower didn't frighten me anymore. I'd seen him turn the same ferocious expression on Joseph when he was upset, not enraged.

"Thank you," I said softly, compelled to convey my gratitude and my newfound trust in him. My belief that he wasn't an evil criminal.

I'd been so blind to his better nature, simmering in resentment over his decision to kidnap me. But when he'd comforted me in the car last night, letting me cry against him as he held me with aching gentleness, I'd finally understood why Joseph cared so much about his intimidating friend.

Fine lines appeared around Marco's mouth on a small frown, and he cocked his head at me.

"Thank you for coming to check on me," I explained. "And for getting me away from…that man." I shuddered at the memory of their enemy's knuckles raking down my cheek in a perversion of intimacy.

Joseph's long, sure fingers trailed through my hair in comforting strokes, and I relaxed into his arms as the last of my residual terror drained from my system. Suddenly, exhaustion sank into my bones, and my head felt too heavy to stir.

The warmth returned to Marco's eyes, and he relaxed, too. "Go back to sleep, princess. I'm right down the hall if you need me. I won't let anyone hurt you."

"I know," I murmured, my eyelids growing heavier with each stroke of Joseph's fingers through my hair. "Thank you."

His answering, low hum followed me down into warm darkness, and I slept peacefully through the night.

Chapter Two
JOSEPH

"I'm going into the city to see my father tonight," I told Marco over breakfast. "I need to talk to him about the threat to Ashlyn. They must've been watching the estate this whole time."

Ashlyn was still sleeping upstairs, likely exhausted from the trauma she'd faced last night.

The memory of her scream tore through my brain. When I'd found that fucker intimidating her in the ladies' room at the restaurant, she'd barely gasped my name. She'd been too frightened to call for my help then, but terror had followed her into her dreams, her nightmares.

If I hadn't gotten worried about her extended absence from our table, if I hadn't gone to check on her...

Rage rushed through me at the thought of that

bastard threatening her, touching her. Ricky Bianchi was easily recognizable by the scar on his cheek. Now, he'd have a broken nose to make him look even uglier.

The fact that I'd bloodied him could cause problems for my father—fighting within the family was forbidden. But Ricky had threatened Ashlyn, so I hoped that balanced out my actions. I didn't want to be the one who instigated war. The threat to Ashlyn had been an intimidation tactic, a power play.

I knew that wouldn't be nearly enough to make my father concede his rightful place as the don's chosen successor. He wouldn't back down because of a few slights and insults. His rival, Gabriel Costa, would literally take power over my father's dead body.

"I agree. You need to tell your father about this," Marco said, his face twisting with fury that matched my own. He'd grown attached to Ashlyn too, despite the fact that she didn't like him.

Attached wasn't a strong enough word. I'd seen the way he'd held her last night. I'd heard him call her *princess.* I knew what that meant.

He was just as obsessed as I was.

I speared him with a significant stare. "I'm having dinner with my dad tonight, so I'll be in the city for several hours. You won't do anything while I'm gone, will you?"

"Like what?" he asked, feigning ignorance.

"You know what. I don't want you to frighten her again. I think she's finally coming around after last night. She's not scared of you anymore. Don't undo the progress we've made."

He frowned. "You're wrong about her. She might look delicate, but she could handle me. She could handle us."

"I swear to god, Marco, don't keep pushing me on this. Back off."

His frown deepened to a scowl, but I saw the hurt flash in his eyes. "You really don't want to share her with me? You really think I'd do something to hurt her?"

I blew out a breath. "I know you'd never hurt her. But you don't understand her. Not like I do."

"I think you're the one who doesn't understand. You're blinded by your obsession with what you think she is. You want her to be this pure, perfect angel who'll save you from your ugly life. She might be pure and perfect, but that doesn't mean she doesn't want you. The *real* you. Stop holding back."

Longing tugged at my chest, and for the first time, doubt crept into my mind. Ever since I'd captured her and told her that I was keeping her, she'd been...different. Sometimes, she seemed like her mind was somewhere else when she was with me.

"You know I'm right," Marco pressed on, reading my hesitation.

I shook my head. "If she's been acting distant sometimes, it's because I haven't earned her trust back yet. It'll take time for her to open up to me again. I betrayed her with my deception."

He cocked his head at me. "And how long has she been acting distant?"

"Since we kidnapped her, obviously."

"She didn't seem distant in those first couple days with you. I saw the way she looked at you. I heard her screaming out her orgasms. Are you sure her distance didn't start a little later? Maybe after she saw my sketches?"

My stomach turned. "If that's the cause, then she's putting distance between us because she's scared of what she saw."

"I don't think so. She wants it, Joseph."

I held up a hand. "Stop this. Just stop. I won't risk scaring her away. I need her, Marco. Don't you get that?"

He sobered, his hard demeanor easing. "Of course I do. I saw how you were without her, and I've seen you together. I know you, Joseph. I get it. But I still think you're wrong about her."

"Then we'll agree to disagree," I declared, tired of the argument. I sighed. "I need to check on Ashlyn. I don't want her to wake up alone."

He nodded, allowing me to close the subject.

I left him in the kitchen and headed upstairs. I planned to spend every minute with Ashlyn before I had to leave. I didn't want to go into the city, not after she'd been threatened, but she'd be safe on the estate. She'd be safe with Marco.

I needed to deal with the threat where it really mattered. If Ashlyn was being targeted, it was actually an attack on my father, an attempt to intimidate us. No one in the family wanted to strike first, so my father's enemies would make subtler power plays until things escalated out of control.

I hoped it wouldn't get to that point, but if they thought they could come anywhere near Ashlyn, I'd do whatever it took to keep her safe.

I opened the bedroom door softly. I didn't want to truly disturb her; she needed to rest. But I at least had to see her, had to touch her. I was addicted to her, just as obsessed as Marco claimed.

I brushed her sable hair back from her face and pressed a soft kiss against her ivory cheek. She let out a happy little humming noise and stretched like a sleepy kitten. She was so adorable, it made my heart ache. I'd be perfectly content to stay here and touch her all day. I'd never get enough of her: her soft body; her sounds of pleasure as I stroked her skin with reverence; her screams of ecstasy when I pinned her down and fucked her hard.

The thought of restraining her burned into my mind, images of her bound in my ropes tormenting me.

No. I shoved the tempting picture from my brain.

The connection we shared was enough to keep me satisfied for ten lifetimes. I could do without my deviant toys as long as I had her in my arms.

"Good morning," she mumbled, her lips curving in a small smile as she opened her pretty blue eyes.

"Good morning, angel. How are you feeling?"

If she was still upset over what had happened last night, I wouldn't leave her side until her fear passed, even if that meant cancelling plans with my father.

A shadow flickered across her eyes, and her brow furrowed. She took in a deep breath and blew it out again. "I'm okay. Marco got me away from that man. And you..." She shivered. "You stopped him."

I didn't like the little shudder that had raced through her.

"What's wrong? Tell me."

Her lashes lowered, hiding her eyes from me. "Would you really... Marco told you not to kill him. Would you have done that?" Her gaze finally lifted, the fear in her eyes cutting into my chest. "Would you have killed him?"

I cupped her face in my hands. She didn't flinch away.

"No. I wouldn't have killed him. I wanted to hurt him, but I wouldn't have killed him."

"Because Marco told you not to?"

"No, angel. Because I don't have it in me." A touch of shame tinged my words as I remembered my father's embarrassment. Even though I didn't want to be a killer, I hated Dad's disappointment.

I took a deep breath and decided to tell her the whole truth, the depth of my sins. I'd owed her this for a long time, and I knew I'd never earn her trust back if she didn't fully understand why I'd run away from New York.

"I have killed a man," I admitted on a pained whisper. "Once. I didn't mean to, but that doesn't change what I did."

Her eyes were wide, but she didn't say anything. She let me continue with my confession.

"When I was younger, a teenager, I was just an errand boy. I helped deliver messages and oversee the exchanges that took place in my family's restaurant, when the drugs changed hands."

That part didn't really bother me. In those days, I'd been eager, ready to make my father proud.

But that was before I learned the realities of my world. My father had shielded me from the violence, wanting me to have a happy childhood.

"That ended when I turned eighteen," I said. "I was a man then, with a man's responsibilities. Marco was in charge of recruiting, finding new men to join our family. I helped him. At first, it was just a matter of identifying boys with a violent streak, boys who wanted to grow into men who moved up in the world and made something of themselves.

"But the jobs got dirtier. Bloodier. I started helping with my father's racketeering, and that involved intimidating people into making deals with our family. When they couldn't pay their debts, Marco and I would threaten them until they did."

I took a deep breath, bracing myself to reveal the ugliest part of my soul.

"About six months ago, we were intimidating a man with the help of some new guys, men Marco and I had recruited."

The victim's name was William Johnston. I'd never forget his name. I'd never forget his face, pale and scared. Bloody and ruined.

"The boys got out of control. They took it too far, and the man ended up in the hospital. He died two days later. And it was my fault."

I grimaced and looked away, no longer able to bear her wide-eyed stare.

"I vomited when I found out. I got sick in front of Dad and Marco's father. My dad was so ashamed of me. I hated that I'd disappointed him, but I hated what I'd done even more. That's why I ran away to Cambridge. I'd always wanted to go to college, but I hadn't been allowed. My education in violence was more important than anything I could learn from a book."

I found her gaze again, desperate to drink her in. This might be the last time she ever allowed me to touch her, and I didn't want to waste a second with her.

"And then I met you, and I deluded myself into believing everything would be okay. That my life would be different. That I'd deserve you."

I traced the lines of her cheekbones with my thumbs. "I know now that I don't. I never will. But I can't let you go, Ashlyn. I need you."

She drew in a sharp breath, but she simply continued to stare up at me in shock.

My gut knotted when she didn't respond right away. "Say something, please," I begged.

She reached up and touched her fingertips to the tense line of my jaw. "I knew you were a good man. I need you too, Joseph."

I huffed out the breath I'd been holding, relief ripping through me.

"I'm not a good man, angel."

Her gaze sharpened with determination. I rarely saw this fire in her, but when it flickered to life, I knew she was about to give me a piece of her formidable mind.

"You are. You didn't ask for your life, and you obviously don't want it. You didn't mean for that man to die."

"That doesn't change the fact that he did," I said, strained.

"No, it doesn't," she allowed. "But the way you feel about it changes everything. When Marco kidnapped me, I thought I didn't know you. I thought I couldn't trust you. But I was always right about you. I know you, Joseph. You *are* a good man. And when all this is over, we'll go back to Cambridge and have the life you want. The life you deserve."

My chest tightened at her words. I wished they were true. I was relieved at her reaction to the ugly truth about me, but I knew her vision of our future was impossible. Now that she was in my world, I wouldn't be able to return her to her old life. Even if she could go back to her classes at Harvard someday, her life would always be tied to mine.

Because I wouldn't let her go. I wasn't capable of letting her go.

"I'd like that, angel," I said, offering her the only truth I could. I longed for the dream of a normal life with her, but the time for that had passed. It had never even been a possibility.

She beamed up at me, elated at my response. She didn't realize that I was deceiving her again, but I couldn't bring myself to shatter this moment with her. By some miracle, she wasn't horrified by the admission that I was a killer. I wasn't willing to ruin that by dashing her hopes. She'd adjust with time, and she'd forget that she'd ever thought about leaving.

I hoped I wasn't deluding myself.

Chapter Three
ASHLYN

"I thought we were going for a walk?" My brow furrowed as Joseph led me into the massive garage, but I didn't hesitate to follow where he led.

His sensual lips tilted in a crooked, heart-stopping smile, and the bright fluorescent light glittered across his aquamarine eyes. "I have something a little more exciting in mind."

His warm hand enfolded mine, tethering me close to his powerful body. He practically glowed with excited anticipation, and I was so entranced by his magnetic energy that I barely noticed the rows of luxury cars, motorcycles, and ATVs.

"Marco lets me keep some of my favorites here," Joseph explained, gesturing toward several vehicles that were probably obscenely expensive. "The storage conditions are ideal, and the garage would be half-empty otherwise. He doesn't really care about cars like I do."

Joseph led me past at least half a dozen sports cars, telling me details about make, model, horsepower, zero-to-sixty, and a lot of other jargon I didn't really understand. He was basically speaking a different language, but I didn't mind one bit. Just seeing him light up with enthusiasm as he gushed about his treasured possessions was brilliant enough to ensnare my full attention.

After several minutes, he paused and shot me a wry grin. "Sorry, I got carried away. Do you know much about cars? I can get pretty geeky about this stuff, and I don't want to bore you."

A giddy laugh bubbled from my chest, his effervescent energy catching. I never would've associated the term *geeky* with gorgeous, self-assured Joseph. But there was something absolutely adorable and achingly endearing about his boyish excitement. This garage was like his own personal playground, and I could listen to him talk about engine types and specs all day, even if I didn't really understand what any of it meant.

"I'm not bored," I promised. "Not at all. I'm happy that you're sharing this with me. It obviously means a lot to you." I went up on my tiptoes and pressed a kiss to his cheek, his rough stubble stimulating my sensitive lips. "And that means a lot to me," I added on a murmur.

I love you. I couldn't say it. Not now. Not yet.

When Marco had kidnapped me and told me that Joseph was a mobster, I'd realized that I didn't really know Joseph at all. But the more time I spent with him on this estate, the more I was coming to understand that maybe I'd known the truth of his soul from the very beginning: Joseph was a good man, and he practically worshipped me.

I locked my deeper feelings for him behind a bright smile, barely managing to contain the confession of love. There was so much I still didn't know about this beautiful, powerful man who'd stormed into my life and swept me off my feet.

But he was sharing with me now. He was showing me not only his deeper nature, but aspects of his personality that made me even more enamored with him. Suddenly, I was greedy to learn everything that Joseph cared about, everything that made him glow like my own personal sun.

"Will you tell me more about what the terminology means?" I asked. "I don't know much about cars, but I'd like to learn."

He lifted our interlocked hands and brushed a kiss over my knuckles. Despite the chaste gesture of affection, his flame-blue eyes blazed with hunger. "We'll start your education in the finer points of auto mechanics some other time. We haven't even gotten to what I really wanted to show you."

He tugged me toward a shiny silver car at the front of the garage. Based on the overall shape of the vehicle, even my untrained eye could tell it was an older model. The lines were slightly blockier than Joseph's other cars, the body crafted in bold planes rather than sensual curves.

His long fingers trailed lovingly over the chrome wing mirror, an echo of the reverent way he caressed my skin when we were in bed together. "This is a '69 Chevy Camaro ZL1. I managed to buy it at auction last year. I've wanted one of these babies since I was sixteen, and now, she's all mine."

"What's so special about this one?" I asked. "What does it do?"

One corner of his sinful mouth ticked up. "This beast has more than five-hundred horsepower, and it's a drag racing legend. Chevy wasn't supposed to put its biggest engine in this model, but a few were manufactured at special request."

His hands suddenly bracketed my hips, and he lifted me to sit on the hood. He stepped in close, forcing my thighs to part. I gasped at the thick, hard bulge pressing against my core. If it weren't for the barriers of his rough jeans and my thin yoga pants, nothing would've prevented him from driving into my slick heat.

My hands clutched at his shoulders, anchoring me to him. His big palm spanned the small of my back and pinned me tighter. His free hand tangled in my hair, fisting the silky locks at my nape. My head tipped back, and I parted my lips in anticipation of his fierce kiss.

But he held me locked in place, restraining me exactly where he wanted me. His gemstone eyes glittered, and his heated words teased across my mouth. "There were only sixty-nine of these '69 Camaro ZL1s ever manufactured. I was a teenager when I first found out about this beauty. What do you think I imagined when I fantasized about owning this car?"

His hips rocked deeper into mine, making his dirty thoughts obvious. It should've been silly to think about Joseph getting hot and bothered over the term *sixty-nine*. But there was nothing silly about his hard body and burning stare, and my blood heated to thrum a sizzling tempo between my legs.

"I'm going to fuck you right here, angel." The low, rumbling promise vibrated against my lips before rolling deeper into my trembling body. "Taking you over the hood of this car is going to surpass every fantasy I've ever managed to imagine." He nipped at my lips, eliciting a gasp as my sensitive nerve endings lit up at the little bite of pain. "Because my brain was never capable of dreaming up anything as perfect as you, Ashlyn." His cock jerked against my core, and he groaned. "Fuck, I need you so bad, angel. You have no idea..."

"I think I do," I insisted breathily, squirming in his restraining hold as I mindlessly sought more stimulation. "I need you too, Joseph. Please..."

He tugged sharply on my hair, forcing me down. He captured my shocked cry on a fierce kiss, the sound of my pained desire mingling with his hungry growl as his tongue surged into my mouth to claim me in harsh, domineering strokes. His massive chest pressed down on mine, and I relished the reassuring weight that both caged and sheltered me.

My pants grew damp with my arousal, and my peaked nipples throbbed for attention. I writhed, struggling to rub the needy buds against his muscular pecs. His big hands captured my wrists, squeezing in reprimand as he pinned them above my head. I whined and wiggled beneath him, becoming drunk on his power over me. Mindlessly, wantonly, I continued to struggle. Not because I wanted to resist him, but because I reveled in the release I found when he exerted his iron control. He took full command of my body, my pleasure. My utter helplessness under his domineering hands sent me flying high, freeing me in a way I never could've imagined before I met him.

My intoxicated haze immediately evaporated when I felt a grating crunch beneath my right shoulder blade. The scratching sound was barely audible, but the harsh scrape resounded in my bones; the small metal clasp on the thin strap of my camisole had gouged a shallow line into the Camaro's shiny silver paint.

I tore my lips from Joseph's on a horrified gasp, my surge of panic intense enough to give me strength to break away.

"Oh my god," I half-moaned. "I scratched your fancy car."

I tried to sit up, struggling in earnest. I couldn't remain on this hood for one more heartbeat in case the thundering against my ribs somehow caused the metal clasp to slip again.

Joseph's sensual lips tugged down in a forbidding frown. Keeping my wrists pinned with one hand, his other settled on my throat. His thumb hooked beneath my jaw to hold my face captive, so I had no choice but to stare up into his stunning eyes. The raw, wild hunger that flared in their pale blue depths drew a shudder from my chest.

Another tiny scratch beneath my shoulder caused my entire body to lock up, and my teeth clenched almost hard enough to crack. "I'm so sorry." I didn't dare release more than a whispered apology.

His dark lashes narrowed. "You think I give a fuck about the paint job?" he demanded, his voice soft and silky smooth. It was somehow more intimidating than if he'd snarled at me. "I want to leave marks of what I'm going to do to you. I want a permanent reminder of how I'm going to fuck you over the hood of this car until you scream my name. And if you keep trying to deny me, I'll force you to come so many times that you'll weep and beg before I finally show mercy."

My core throbbed with a painful ache as relentless desire pulsed through me in response to his sensual threat. The wave of lust was so intense that my thighs shook around his hips. His hard length jerked, and he bit out a curse.

A whimper slipped up my throat as the tiny metal clasps on my camisole marred the paint a third time. No matter how hot Joseph's dirty words made me, I couldn't shake the spike of guilt at every scratch. He'd wanted this car since he was sixteen years old. There were only sixty-nine ZL1s like it in existence.

My teeth sank into my lower lip. Joseph was almost feral with desire right now, but what about later? Once this lust-drunk fever passed, he might regret the damage.

His dark brows drew together in a forbidding slash. "Stop worrying, angel. I want to leave these marks. I got this baby for just under a million at auction, but it'll be infinitely more valuable to me after I finish with you today."

"*A million dollars?!*" I squeaked, starting to freak out.

This was too much. It was insane to even contemplate devaluing the rare car further, no matter what Joseph said. There was no way he wouldn't regret this later.

He cocked his head at me, his burning gaze tracing the taut, anxious lines of my drawn features. After several breathless seconds, he gave me a tight nod.

"You just need to get in the right headspace," he declared, decisive. "I can fix that."

Cold air slapped my skin when he suddenly stood, separating our heated bodies. I stared at him for a moment, stunned at his capitulation. I'd expected my unyielding lover to forcibly seduce me, not back off.

I hastily pushed off the hood before he could change his mind, shivering at the coolness that kissed my burning flesh.

Joseph immediately wrapped a corded arm around me, rubbing his calloused hand over my pebbled skin.

I leaned into him, addicted to his warmth and strength.

"We're going for a little joyride," he informed me, ushering me to the passenger seat. "Once we get your adrenaline pumping, you'll be too giddy to worry about anything other than pleasing me."

The velvety words enfolded me: a promise and a warning. Joseph had been demanding in bed before, and our sexual relationship had become more deviant since he'd brought me to the estate. But something darker had settled over him, something that made me tremble even as it tempted me.

When he directed me to slide into the white leather seat, his hands lingered around my body. He drew the seatbelt over my chest and around my waist. Once I was securely buckled in place, he fisted the belt at my shoulder and side, pulling the straps tight. My head dropped back on a moan at the feel of the firm restraints; both thrilling and perversely comforting. Wordlessly, Joseph reminded me that he was still fully in control of my body, even if he had paused his wickedest intentions for me.

His crystalline eyes sparkled, mesmerizing me. His entrancing stare glowed with something between awe and fierce possessiveness, and my breath stuttered as his power completely overwhelmed me.

When I was practically quivering, he finally

pulled away with a satisfied smirk. He shut my door before prowling around the car, all predatory grace as he crossed to the wall where dozens of keys hung in neat rows. He snagged the ones he needed and returned, pressing a button on the keyring as he slid into the driver's seat.

The huge garage doors began to lift, and the midday sunlight poured inside to glint over the Camaro's shiny silver paint. I winced at the sight of the tiny scratches on the hood, but Joseph immediately snagged my full attention. He revved the engine, and the car snarled like a beast pacing at the bars of its cage. The fierce rumble made the Camaro vibrate almost violently, and the sensation rolled relentlessly through my core.

His cruelly pleased grin was sharp enough to cut into my chest and rob my breath.

I wiggled in my seat, and his low chuckle only added to the rumbling between my legs. He wasn't even touching me, but still he toyed with me, keeping me firmly in his thrall.

I was still staring at him with my lips parted when he slammed down on the gas. My shocked shriek was lost in the squeal of the tires against asphalt, and the beast lurched forward, leaving my stomach a few seconds behind.

The sudden surge of speed made my head spin,

the insanely rapid acceleration beyond disorienting. My hands scrambled for something solid, and my fingers locked around the sides of the leather seat.

Joseph's delighted laugh boomed through the car, flooding the small space with rich, pure joy that was more powerful than the roaring engine.

I tore my eyes from the dizzying blur of greenery outside and focused on him. He glowed with the same excited energy that'd emanated from him in the garage, but exponentially brighter. His gaze was fixed on the long, straight driveway as he handled the car with the confidence of years of experience. He wasn't chuckling with wicked amusement anymore; his carefree laugh was a sound of almost childlike thrill. I stared at his handsome profile, utterly entranced by this incandescent display of happiness.

When he was in my arms, I'd seen Joseph both peacefully content and darkly pleased. But now, he was allowing me to see the purest parts of his heart. The sight of his unabashed joy warmed me all the way down to my toes, and a giddy laugh bubbled from my own chest as his levity swept me up along with him.

His wide, silly grin broadened, but he didn't take his eyes from the road to glance in my direction. Even though we were going so fast that I didn't dare check the speedometer, a sense of safety wrapped around me. Joseph wouldn't risk me for even one second by diverting his attention.

"Brace yourself, angel. Ready to drift?"

He didn't give me a chance to respond before turning the rosewood steering wheel sharply to the left. I squealed along with the tires as the back end of the car spun out at the speedy turn.

My shriek broke into a delighted laugh that danced with Joseph's as he leaned into the turn, steering us around the enormous fountain at the center of the circular driveway in front of the mansion.

Acrid smoke from the burning rubber tires billowed around us, but sudden movement to the right of the speeding car caught my attention. Through the gray haze, I made out Marco's hulking form storming from the mansion. He waved his brawny arms over his head, and his mouth moved as though he was shouting. I couldn't hear his words over the roar of the engine, but the harsh tilt of his dark brows and his rippling muscles clearly communicated fury.

Joseph must've spotted him too, because the car slowed. Despite the obvious immediacy of Marco's inaudible shouting, Joseph ensured that I didn't so much as jolt in my seat as we rolled to a gentle stop.

The car had barely stopped moving before Marco

was at my door. He wrenched it open and leaned over me to unbuckle my seatbelt. Rage tensed his every movement, but his massive hands were gentle on my waist as he lifted me out of the car and carefully set me down on my feet.

Once I found my balance, he didn't withdraw his touch. Everything was happening so fast that my brain couldn't catch up, and I stared at him in silent bewilderment as his hands glided over my body, checking every inch of me. His flinty black eyes raked across my skin, leaving fiery trails in their wake.

"Are you okay, princess?" he murmured, his voice as smooth and gentle as his hands. The contradiction of his tenderness with his ferocity was almost hypnotic.

The slam of Joseph's car door snapped me back to full awareness, and I jolted away from Marco. Shock blanked my mind again when his corded arm settled over my shoulders, and his bulky frame practically curved around me like a protective shield.

"What the hell were you thinking?" he snarled at Joseph.

I tried to edge away, but his massive arm flexed around me. He wasn't holding me harshly, but the warning to stay put was clear.

Joseph stomped towards us, his eyes chips of blue ice. "What the fuck, Marco? Back off."

Marco's blocky jaw hardened to granite, and he fixed his sharp, obsidian stare on the man I loved.

I shifted, uneasy in his iron grip. He didn't even seem to register my small show of resistance; his full, furious attention remained riveted on Joseph.

"Are you insane?" he barked. "You know how dangerous that shit is. You shouldn't be drag racing with Ashlyn in the car."

Joseph halted mere feet from us, rocking back slightly as though he'd hit a brick wall. He sucked in a hissed breath between his clenched teeth, and he managed to restrain himself from physically removing me from his friend's arms.

"I know what I'm doing," Joseph seethed. "You know I'm an experienced driver. And I'd never risk Ashlyn."

"He didn't take his eyes off the road for even a second," I chimed in, my voice oddly small and high-pitched. "I didn't feel unsafe at all. I was having fun."

Joseph shot me a grateful half-smile, and my swift defense of his actions seemed to melt most of his icy anger toward his friend.

His posture relaxed slightly when he turned his attention back on Marco. "I get why you're upset. Seriously, I do. I should've let you know what I planned before we took a joyride."

"It was a spontaneous thing," I added quickly.

"That wasn't what we were..."

I trailed off, my cheeks burning. I was so intent on defusing the situation that I'd almost blabbed to Marco about what Joseph had really wanted to do with me in the garage.

Joseph's smile took on a wicked twist, but he kept his focus on his friend's thunderous expression. "I'd never put Ashlyn at risk. You know that, right?"

Marco's hard features remained stony for several more heartbeats, but eventually, he drew in a shaky breath. His onyx eyes turned on me, bottomless dark pools that threatened to swallow me up.

"You really are okay, princess?" His voice took on that achingly tender tone again.

I nodded, eager to reassure him.

He blew out a heavy sigh, and his big hand brushed up and down my arm once before he finally released me.

"Lunch will be ready in fifteen minutes," he announced before turning on his heel and stalking into the house.

I jumped when Joseph's warm hand spanned the small of my back. "Sorry about that, angel. I should've realized Marco might freak out about racing if I didn't give him advance warning." He shot me a crooked smile that made my toes curl. "You make it difficult to think straight sometimes."

I winced, remembering his reckless disregard for the scratches on his precious car. My eyes had barely darted to the shiny silver hood before he hooked his thumb beneath my jaw and captured my face. He forced me to meet his glittering gaze, commanding my full attention.

"We're going to finish ruining that paint job later," he swore. "And if I hear even one word of protest about scratching the car—if your pretty little body even tenses up with worry—I'll make you suffer that much longer before I finally show mercy."

His dark promise teased over my sensitized flesh, stimulating my senses like a caress. The almost painful desire he'd awakened in me when he'd pinned me to the hood of the car began to stir once again.

He brushed a quick, regretful kiss over my lips before stepping away. "Later," he said firmly, as though speaking to himself as much as to me. "I don't think Marco could hold his temper in check if we get anywhere near that car again today. I'd hate to ruin the experience if he came storming back out here and ripped me off you."

My brow furrowed. I didn't understand why Joseph was being so weirdly accepting of his friend's overbearing aggression. "Would he really be that upset?"

The lust drained from Joseph's eyes, and his

mouth took on a sad twist. "Marco was in a serious accident when he was seventeen. He wrapped his Ferrari around a tree and was in the hospital for a week. He's always been cool with my drag racing, but I should've anticipated that he'd freak about you being in the car with me. I know he seems scary when he gets intense like that, but he was actually scared. But don't tell him that I told you that."

"About the accident, or about the fact that he was scared?" Joseph had always kept Marco's secrets before, rebuffing my questions about some of his strangest behavior—like his refusal to get the pool filled for me. Maybe it wasn't okay that Joseph was sharing this more intimate admission about his friend without his knowledge.

"Both. I'm telling you this because I don't want you to be afraid of him, but he probably wouldn't want you to know about that stuff. And if he did, he'd want to tell you himself."

I nodded, understanding. Marco was a hard man in a hard world. He'd shown me a shockingly tender facet of his personality, but he probably wasn't used to betraying any vulnerability. Maybe not even to Joseph.

"I'm not afraid of him," I declared. "Not anymore."

"You're not?" Joseph looked skeptical, but hopeful. "I know that was pretty intense, how he pulled you out of the car like that."

"He was just worried about my safety," I countered. "I get that now. He came to check on me when I had that nightmare, and he got me away from that man at the restaurant last night." I swallowed down the flutter of fear elicited by the memory of the scarred man's hand on my face. "If Marco was in a bad car accident as a teen, I can understand how that might've made his reaction a little irrational. Trauma can bring out strong emotions, especially if you're not prepared for a possible trigger." I squeezed Joseph's hand. "Thank you for sharing that with me. It helps me understand. I know Marco just wants to protect me."

Joseph pressed a kiss to my forehead. "I'm glad to hear that, angel."

I offered him a bright smile, putting the disconcerting encounter firmly behind us. "We should probably go inside. Marco will be annoyed if we're late for lunch."

Joseph chuckled. "You're definitely starting to understand him." He shot one last, regretful glance at the Camaro in the driveway. "But I *will* be fucking you over the hood of that car later, and we're going to mark the ever-living hell out of the paint."

Chapter Four
MARCO

"Is your lasagna okay?" I asked, breaking the stretch of silence. Ashlyn was pushing her food around her plate rather than eating it. She'd been quiet ever since Joseph had left to go into the city half an hour ago.

Apparently, whatever they'd been up to in the garage before their idiotic joyride had made him lose track of time; he'd practically bolted out the door when he'd entered the kitchen for lunch and caught sight of the clock. He couldn't be late to the meeting with his dad, no matter how difficult it was to separate himself from Ashlyn. Dominic had to be informed about how Ricky Bianchi had threatened her. Warning Joseph's dad about the danger to her was the most important thing right now.

So, that left me alone with the gorgeous brunette,

just the two of us seated at the kitchen island to eat the meal I'd prepared. I'd anticipated having her all to myself for the afternoon and evening, but I hadn't expected this shy silence.

She glanced up at me, her lovely eyes flashing like sapphires before her gaze dropped back to her plate. "The lasagna's great. Thanks for cooking for me all the time. You don't have to do that."

It was the first time she'd ever expressed gratitude for my cooking. Something swelled in my chest.

"I want to do it," I told her. "I like cooking for you."

I'd like to take care of her more, if she'd let me.

My gut told me she'd welcome Joseph's kinkier games. I wanted her to welcome me, too.

But my perversions weren't a game. They were a part of me, a need that gnawed at my soul. In the time she'd been with us, that need had shifted to Ashlyn. I'd thought about her countless times, our few intense encounters giving me enough fantasies to make me come in the shower every day. When I stroked myself, I'd close my eyes and remember the way she trembled for me.

She might think her reactions were fearful, but I knew better. She was a little intimidated, but she liked when I imposed myself on her. I could see it in the way her eyes locked on mine and her breathing hitched as she stared up at me. When I turned that side of myself on her, I commanded her full attention.

And when I'd held her in the car last night, protecting her and sheltering her while she cried, I knew I was just as devoted to her as Joseph was.

Three times in less than twenty-four hours, I'd been wracked by fear for her safety: first when I found Ricky cornering her in that bathroom; then when she'd screamed during her nightmare; and just this afternoon, when I'd caught sight of Joseph drag racing with her in the damn car.

And she'd softened toward me each time I'd rushed to protect her, instinctively trusting me to keep her safe.

The intense bursts of emotion had totally fucked with my head. I'd promised Joseph that I wouldn't push her. I'd promised that he could have her, and I wouldn't press my claim.

He might secretly want to corrupt her innocence, but I would cherish it. I'd ensure that she never lost that part of herself, no matter how depraved Joseph's games became. She was made for both of us, a perfect match for our needs.

I just needed to convince Joseph that I was right.

"You're not eating," I observed. "Are you still upset about what happened with Ricky at the restaurant last night? You know I won't let him anywhere near you ever again, don't you?"

She peeked up at me. "I know. But I do feel...a little out of sorts. It would really help if I could go for a swim." Her tone turned hopeful, and her eyes were wide and beseeching. "It helps clear my mind."

I locked down my emotions before they could rise, shoving them away with familiar, ruthless force.

"No," I said, an absolute refusal. I'd been putting Joseph off, but I had no intention of getting that pool filled and letting Ashlyn in the water. "Now, eat your lunch."

Her brows rose. "*No?* That's it? Just *no?*"

I placed my hands on the marble countertop, leaning toward her. The kitchen island separated us, but she shrank back on her stool.

"That's it. *No.* Now, eat."

Her lips thinned, her eyes flashing. "*No,*" she said, the word heavy with mockery. She flung her fork down. It clattered on the china plate.

I fixed her with my sternest stare. "I'm going to give you three seconds to pick up that fork and eat, little girl."

"*Little girl?*" she repeated, her voice high and thin. Her cheeks flushed with something other than anger.

I tipped my head in confirmation. "That's right. Now, be a good girl and eat the meal I made for you."

Her lips parted on a disbelieving huff. I was certain no one had ever talked to her like this. She'd probably been spoiled, cosseted. Joseph certainly treated her with kid gloves.

She wouldn't get that from me. She'd get a firm hand and learn a little respect.

She pushed her stool back from the island and got to her feet, flipping her long hair over her shoulder as she turned away from me. "You're being ridiculous."

"And you're being a brat."

To my shock, she shot me the middle finger and started storming off.

Any restraint I might have possessed snapped. I'd held back, for Joseph.

I was done denying who I was. I was done denying what I wanted.

It only took three long strides for me to catch up with her and close my hand around her upper arm.

"Let me go," she seethed.

"*No*," I said again, mocking her this time. "You want to be a brat? You'll get treated like a brat."

I grasped her waist and bent slightly so I could lift her over my shoulder. She shrieked and kicked out. I barely felt the little blows of her knees on my abs. She really was small and delicate, but I knew she could take what I needed to do to her.

Her fists pounded against my back, feeling more like a massage than angry punches.

I started striding up the stairs, eager to get her back to my bedroom.

She twisted on my shoulder, but holding her in place was laughably easy.

"Put me down!" she demanded.

I savored the little quaver in her voice as I stepped into the bedroom. I set her down on her feet, and she tried to shove at my chest. I grasped her wrists in one hand, pulling her toward the corner. I pressed her hands against the wall, so she was facing away from me. Then, I pushed my chest against her back, letting her feel my presence. I was careful to keep my hips away from hers, though. She wasn't ready to feel my hard-on. Not yet.

She stopped yelling at me, going quiet except for her little panting breaths.

"You want to act like a brat?" I growled in her ear. "Brats get punished. Brats get disciplined."

She shivered. "What are you—"

I nipped at her neck, a sharp bite of rebuke. "Quiet, little girl. You're in enough trouble as it is."

I kept her wrists pinned with one hand, leaning against her back so she was forced to press her chest to the wall.

"Stay still and take your punishment like a good

girl," I rumbled in her ear before brushing a kiss over the spot I'd bitten.

"Are you…" Her voice broke. "Please, don't hurt me."

I nuzzled my cheek against hers, letting her feel our connection. "I'm not going to hurt you, princess. You're going to have a very sore bottom when I'm finished with you, but I won't hurt you. Do you understand?"

"No, I don't," she whispered, her small body shaking.

"I think you do," I countered. "You've practically been begging me for a spanking ever since you got here. You're not a brat with Joseph, are you? You only act out around me. Because you know I'll give you what you need."

"And what's that?" she asked tremulously, but she wasn't struggling to get away from me.

"Discipline. Structure. Rules. You need someone who will take care of you, someone who cares enough to correct your behavior when you're acting out for attention."

"I don't want attention."

"Don't you?" I challenged. "I know you care about Joseph, but he's not giving you what you need. I'll give you what you need."

"You're scaring me," she breathed, but she still wasn't trying to fight me off.

"You're not scared, princess. You've never been scared of me. Not really. You're scared of what you want from me. You're scared of how I make you feel."

I wrapped my arm around her and cupped her breast, squeezing gently. She gasped and arched into my touch.

"And I'm going to make you feel so good, babygirl. I promise. But first, you need a lesson in respect. You've been pushing me, testing me. Then, you hide behind Joseph before I can give you what you really want. Well, I'm not going to let him come between us anymore. He's acting like an idiot, and I've run out of patience. You shouldn't have flipped me off, princess. That was very naughty. You should have been a good girl and eaten the meal I made for you."

"I didn't want to." There it was. The petulant pout I'd been waiting for. She was playing right into my hands, even if she didn't realize what was happening between us.

"It doesn't matter that you didn't want to. Daddy knows what's best for you."

"What?" The question was barely audible, coming out on a little puff of air.

"You heard me, little girl." I palmed her breast, and her head tipped back against my shoulder. "I don't have many rules, but the most important one is that you always respect Daddy."

"I... I don't know what you're talking about." The words were faint, breathless.

"You will. I have so much to teach you, princess." I pulled back just far enough so she'd feel the heat of my declaration on her neck. "You will learn. I'm going to punish you now. I'm going to turn your pretty bottom red with my hand. You're going to take your discipline like a good girl, aren't you?"

"I... I don't know..."

I shushed her gently. "You'll feel better after. You shouldn't have flipped me off. You know it was wrong, don't you?"

"I was mad at you. You aren't going to let me use the pool."

"We can't always get what we want, babygirl. You have to trust that Daddy knows what's best for you. It's not okay to disrespect me, even if you're mad."

I moved my hand down from her breast, feeling her body through the thin camisole she wore. When I reached the band of her yoga pants, I tugged the material down slowly, revealing her bare ass.

Fuck. Joseph hadn't given her underwear.

Maybe he wasn't holding back as much as I'd thought.

I pushed the pants down her thighs, leaving them

bunched at her knees so she couldn't kick out at me, if she decided to be even naughtier.

I didn't think she would, though. My princess was a sweet girl at heart. She just needed attention. Correction. Affection.

I lightly tapped my palm against her pale ass cheek, just hard enough to elicit a small *pop*. Judging by way she gasped and rocked her hips forward, you'd think I'd put my full strength behind the blow.

I wrapped my arm around her waist, guiding her back so her ass was thrust out, waiting for my discipline.

"Stay still," I commanded, my tone dropping deeper without a thought.

A light tremor ran through her body, but she didn't shift away when I released her waist.

I stroked her ass, letting her feel the heat and size of my hand. "Good girl."

She pressed her face against her arm and let out the most adorable little whimper. She was deeply affected by my words of praise, by my gentle touch. She was still confused, probably overwhelmed by her reaction to the shifting dynamic between us.

But she wasn't moving away from my hand.

My cock throbbed, straining against my jeans.

I took a breath and mastered my lust for her. This was for her benefit, not my sexual gratification. I got a deeper satisfaction out of her budding acceptance than I could have attained from a rough fuck against the wall.

"I'm going to give you ten," I told her. "I want you to count them. Can you do that for me, princess?"

She kept her face tucked against her arm, as though she could hide from what was happening between us. But she nodded, and I was satisfied that she was ready to continue. She wasn't screaming at me to let her go. She wasn't fighting.

She was submitting, and her surrender was the hottest fucking thing I'd ever experienced.

I let the first stinging slap land. It was little more than a love tap, but she wasn't accustomed to this. She'd probably never been spanked in her life, as a child or an adult. So, I'd get her warmed up. I'd go a little easy on her. This first time, at least.

"You're supposed to count," I reminded her.

"One," she whispered.

I slapped her other cheek, spreading out the heat.

"Two."

The third hit was harder, delivering a little more sting. I watched her, studying her reaction.

"Three."

Her face was still against her arm, her eyes squeezed shut.

I resumed stroking her ass. "Look at me." It was an order, but my tone was soft, cajoling.

Her lashes fluttered, revealing her pretty blue eyes. She looked at me with such innocent confusion that all the air was knocked from my chest. She was just as pure and perfect as Joseph had always said, and I now fully understood why he worshipped her.

I tucked her hair behind her ear, and she didn't flinch from my touch.

"You're doing so well, babygirl. So sweet, trusting me to take care of you."

"But you're spanking me," she whispered. She still didn't understand her feelings. Deep in her heart, she knew this was a form of caretaking. But her feminist sensibilities were telling her that this was wrong.

"I am." I trailed my fingers through her hair. "And you're being so good for me. Are you sorry you disrespected me?"

She nodded, and I saw the truth in her eyes: she really meant it. She wasn't lying to get out of further punishment.

"We'll make it five, then," I conceded. "Just this once. But don't expect me to go soft on you every time. Consistency is important, and know that I'll always follow through."

She nodded again, accepting.

My cock jerked toward her, my balls aching. I bit back a groan and focused on what I needed to do.

"Two more, and then I want to hear you apologize," I told her.

"But I am sorry," she said softly.

I gave her a small smile. "I know you are. Two more. Don't forget to count."

I slapped her twice in quick succession, hard and precise. She shrieked and squirmed, trying to move away from the sting I'd inflicted.

"Four," she gasped. "Five."

"Such a good girl. Are you ready to apologize?"

"I'm sorry." She tucked her face against her arm again, her cheeks as red as her ass.

I clicked my tongue at her, calling her attention back to me. I rested my hand against her bottom, letting her feel the warning.

"Look me in the eye, and tell me again."

Her gorgeous eyes met mine. They were no longer clouded with confusion, but they shone with tears. I hadn't spanked her hard enough to make her cry. These tears were cathartic, and I'd never seen anything so beautiful.

"I'm sorry."

"*Daddy*," I prompted, lightly squeezing her ass.

"I'm sorry, Daddy." She mumbled the words, still embarrassed by what was happening.

I pressed a kiss against her forehead. "I forgive you. I think my good girl has earned a reward. Are you wet for me, princess?"

She didn't answer, but I knew the truth before I dipped my fingers between her legs. I could already smell her arousal, and when I touched her inner thighs, I found her soaking wet for me.

I growled my satisfaction and kissed her forehead again. "Come for Daddy, princess."

"I can't."

"Of course you can. You're dripping all over my hand."

She shook her head, but I read the need in her wide eyes.

"You don't have to be scared, babygirl. I'm right here. I've got you. And I want you to give me a nice, big orgasm."

I rubbed my thumb over her hard little clit, and she cried out. I still had her wrists pinned to the wall above her head, but she didn't try to escape. Instead, she rotated her hips toward my touch, seeking more stimulation.

I obliged her, easing two fingers into her tight cunt. She whimpered as I filled her, and when I found the sensitive spot at the front of her inner walls, a shudder wracked her body.

"Come for me," I urged, coaxing rather than

ordering. She was vulnerable, still confused by her reaction to me and the connection between us.

I curled my fingers against her g-spot and rubbed her clit with my thumb. She shattered on a scream, and her pussy gripped my fingers. If my cock had been inside her, it would've been enough to make me lose all control. As it was, the sight of her squirming on my hand while she rode out her orgasm was the hottest thing I'd ever experienced. It took effort to prevent myself from coming in my pants.

I wanted her. I wanted to take her, fuck her, make her mine.

But she wasn't ready for that. If I fucked her right now, I'd be taking advantage of her in a vulnerable state. I needed her fully aware and consenting before I could use her body the way I wanted to.

When she started to whine from sensitivity, I withdrew my hand. I lifted my wet fingers to my lips and sucked them clean. She tasted every bit as decadent as I'd dreamed. And the way she watched my crude behavior with those wide, doe eyes...

Fuck.

I released her hands and spun her around to face me. My fingers sank into her hair, tipping her head back so I could capture her lips with mine. She opened for me on a shocked gasp, and I thrust my tongue inside her hot mouth, allowing myself to show her how I wanted to drive my cock into her pretty pussy.

Her hands came up to press against my chest, but she wasn't pushing me away. She softened against me, allowing me to deepen the kiss. I knew she could taste her wet desire that lingered on my tongue from when I'd cleaned my fingers, but she didn't pull away in disgust. She allowed me to claim her with possessive strokes. I kissed her without finesse, taking what I so desperately needed from her.

I'd known I wanted her from the moment I first saw her. But when I heard my name on her lips —*Daddy*—I was lost. I'd do anything for her, fall at her feet and worship her, just like Joseph did.

She was mine, my perfect little princess.

Now, I just had to convince Joseph to make her his dirty little angel.

I'd been right: Ashlyn was made for us. Both of us.

Chapter Five

ASHLYN

Shock blanked my mind. I couldn't think, couldn't process what I'd done. What I'd allowed Marco to do to me. He'd finally freed me from his possessive kiss, and he was holding me tight. My face was tucked against his chest, my cheeks still burning.

I realized my fingers were fisted in his shirt, clinging to him like I had when he'd protected me in the car last night.

I forced them to unfurl. My stomach dropped when I released him, but I ignored the sensation.

"I..." I swallowed and tried to collect my thoughts. "I need to take a shower."

Yes. That sounded like a good idea. The evidence of my orgasm was slick on my thighs, and I needed to clean up. I needed to erase the evidence.

My stomach knotted, and I shied away from my budding realization of the horrible betrayal I'd just committed.

He kissed the top of my head. "Okay, babygirl. Take a shower. You can study after, and I'll bring you dinner later."

I nodded, numbness setting in.

He finally released me from his strong arms, and goosebumps pebbled my skin at the loss of his heat.

"Go on," he prompted when I didn't budge.

I moved quickly, tearing myself away from him like ripping off a Band-Aid. I rushed to the bathroom and closed the door behind me to put a barrier between us.

Moving on auto-pilot, I removed my clothes and turned on the shower. I kept the water little more than lukewarm. My body was hot, flushed from my orgasm. I needed to cool off.

Orgasm. I'd come all over Marco's hand, driven to the height of pleasure by his deep voice and demanding touch. I'd felt small in his grip, helpless to resist him.

But the awful truth was I hadn't been helpless. He hadn't violated me against my will. I might have been confused by what was happening, but I'd still been an active participant.

I'd kissed him back.

After he made me come. After he spanked me. After he made me call him *Daddy*.

Shame rolled through me in nauseating waves.

I cheated on Joseph. I cheated on Joseph with his best friend.

The thought was enough to make my stomach lurch, and bile crept up my throat. I took a deep breath through my nose and suppressed the urge to vomit.

I locked down my roiling emotions before they could rise. I couldn't cope with the enormity of what I'd done. The weight of my betrayal would crush my heart if I faced it.

Take a shower. You can study after. Marco's words echoed in my head, perversely comforting. If I just did what he'd told me to do, I could zone out and continue to exist for a little while longer. Once Joseph returned to me, I'd have to confess my horrific sin, and my heart would shatter.

After he'd opened up to me about his crimes this morning, about the man who had died because of his actions, I'd been ready to trust him again. I'd almost been ready to say *I love you*.

Now, that was ruined. How could I possibly tell him I loved him when I'd just cheated with Marco?

I shuddered and turned up the heat of the water. My skin was suddenly far too chilled.

I stayed in the shower for a long time, allowing the scalding water to beat down on me until I couldn't stand it anymore.

When I was dry and dressed in fresh clothes, I moved back out into the bedroom and settled myself at the desk. I opened the notes my classmate had uploaded for me. Marco had printed them out—I still hadn't been granted access to the internet, even though I'd been allowed to write a few more emails to Jayme. My father hadn't even deigned to reply to my first message about taking time off from school, so there had been no need to send him any more emails.

I shied away from that fresh layer of pain. My heart couldn't take it.

I was letting down everyone I loved. I was a failure, a traitor. A disappointment.

I swiped away a stray tear and focused on the notes, trying to absorb the information. If I could just succeed at academics, maybe I could at least win my father's affection back.

For hours, I stared at the pages before me, slowly flipping through them before backtracking to try to actually read the words I'd been glossing over.

I jolted when the bedroom door opened. Marco hadn't bothered to knock.

I didn't look at him, but I could feel his approach. He set down a glass of water and a perfectly golden grilled cheese beside my notes. A thick, dark chocolate brownie was plated separately, delicately dusted with powdered sugar.

"You didn't eat enough at lunch, princess. I know it's a little early for dinner, but you must be hungry."

I nodded, a rote motion. I wasn't hungry. I was just...empty.

He tucked my hair behind my ear, and I flinched. He withdrew slowly. I could feel the weight of his eyes considering me, but I kept my gaze glued to my notes.

He sighed. "I'll be back for those plates in half an hour. I expect them to be empty. Do you understand?"

He was using that authoritative tone again. So, I nodded my agreement.

Another beat of heavy silence passed before his footsteps retreated. Moving as though in a dream, I ate the sandwich. It was perfect; just crispy enough, with at least four types of gooey cheese inside. The flavors were comforting, and I devoured the whole thing in a matter of minutes without thinking.

The decadent brownie should've been cloying on my acid tongue, but even though I was devastated, I couldn't deny the allure of chocolate.

When I was finished, I went back to staring at my notes.

Marco came to retrieve the plates a while later. His murmured "good girl" made a thread of warmth curl in my chest, but it did little to ease the chill inside.

Time passed. I went through the notes again, flipping the pages every few minutes to give myself something to do.

I didn't realize that night was falling until Marco came and flipped on the light. I blinked against the sudden illumination, but I kept my eyes downcast when he approached.

"It's time to put your notes away. Brush your teeth and get ready for bed," he ordered.

It seemed early for that, but I wasn't really doing anything, anyway. Sleep sounded like a good idea.

I nodded again.

I did as he instructed, and a while later, my mouth tasted minty fresh as I tucked myself under the duvet. The silky pink nightgown Joseph had bought for me glided across my skin as I moved, but I barely registered the lush sensation. I closed my eyes and drifted, somewhere between sleep and wakefulness.

Sometime later, the soft *click* of the bedside lamp turning on roused me. I rolled onto my back and opened my eyes to find Joseph looking down at me, a small smile curving his sensual lips.

"Hey, angel. I missed you."

A harsh sob tore from my chest, and I turned my face into the pillow. I couldn't face him. I couldn't confess what I'd done. I couldn't lose him.

He shushed me gently and sat on the bed. His strong arms closed around me, lifting me so I rested against his chest. He rubbed his hand up and down my back, trying to soothe me.

Once I confessed, he would never hold me again. I sobbed harder, clinging to him.

"I'm sorry," I forced out. "I'm so sorry."

"It's okay," he said gently, continuing to stroke and comfort me. "You're okay. Don't cry, angel."

"But I... You don't know..." I choked on the words, unable to voice the depth of my betrayal.

"Marco told me what happened. It's okay."

My next sob caught in my throat. I blinked hard to clear my tears away. I peered up at him to read his expression.

"What?" I asked thickly.

He smoothed my hair back from my forehead. "It's okay," he said again. "I know what happened, and it's okay."

I shook my head. "You don't understand," I said, each word causing pain to knife through my chest. "I kissed him back."

"I know. And I'm not upset with you, angel."

My breath stuttered. I could hardly dare to

believe it. "So, you don't... You don't hate me? You forgive me?"

How could it be so easy? If Joseph had touched another woman, I'd be heartbroken.

"Of course I don't hate you. There's nothing to forgive."

My brow furrowed. I didn't understand. How could he not care? He'd been so fiercely possessive of me when we'd first met. He still was. I could feel it in the desperate way he kissed me.

"You aren't angry?"

Impossibly, he gave me a dazzling smile. "You make me very happy, angel."

"So, you... You still want to be with me?"

"Always," he promised. "We want to be with you. Both of us."

My heart fluttered. Surely, I hadn't heard him correctly. "Both of you?" My question was little more than a squeak.

He nodded. "Both of us. Marco and me."

"But I can't... That's not..." I stammered, unable to form a coherent sentence. I couldn't even formulate a coherent thought. I was suddenly far too hot in Joseph's arms.

"I told you I was right about her." Marco's voice rumbled over me, drawing my attention like a magnet. "Look at that pretty blush."

He stood in the doorway, watching me intently.

Joseph's fingers trailed over my heated cheek, and electricity danced across my skin. My body hummed with awareness. I could feel Marco's presence as keenly as I could feel Joseph's physical touch.

"You were right," Joseph agreed with him. "I should have listened."

My head was spinning, and I felt oddly disconnected from my thoughts. Everything was surreal, as though this was a strange dream.

"But I cheated on you," I told Joseph on a pained whisper.

"It's not like that with Marco and me." He was bizarrely calm. "I'm happy that you opened up to Marco."

I stared at him, disbelieving. I must have drifted off, after all, because this couldn't be reality.

"Kiss her, Joseph," Marco commanded. "She doesn't believe you. Show her how you feel."

My gaze redirected to Joseph, gauging his reaction to being ordered around by Marco in this strange way.

Joseph's aquamarine eyes burned with lust, and he leaned in to capture my lips with his.

Definitely a dream, I decided. There was no way Joseph would forgive me for cheating on him with Marco, and he certainly wouldn't kiss me like I was the most precious thing in his world. He held me carefully, cradling me in his arms as his mouth caressed mine.

I decided to relax into the pleasant fantasy my mind had conjured. I tipped my head back, welcoming him to claim me more deeply. When his tongue swept into my mouth, I moaned in relief.

He doesn't hate me. At least, this dream version of Joseph didn't hate me.

A big hand closed around mine.

Marco. I recognized the feel of him now: his palms were slightly rougher than Joseph's, his fingers thicker.

He used his gentle grip on my hand to guide my touch. My palm rasped against jeans, and I gasped into Joseph's mouth. I was familiar with this, too: the feel of his hard cock straining toward me.

"Feel how much he wants you," Marco said. "Feel how much he wants this. How much he wants *us*. Together. All of us."

Joseph's cock jerked beneath my hand, and he groaned against me. His fist tangled in my hair, and his teeth nipped at my lower lip, lighting up my nerve endings with a little hit of pain.

"That's it," Marco urged, his voice like dark velvet. "Stop treating her like she's made of glass. She can take it. She can take both of us."

I shuddered in Joseph's arms, erotic tension rolling through me with visceral force. My pussy was wet and throbbing for attention, and he'd barely touched me.

They'd barely touched me.

Oh, god.

They were both touching me. Joseph and Marco.

And this didn't feel like a dream.

This was wrong. Marco shouldn't be here. I was supposed to belong to Joseph.

But Marco didn't give me time to think about protesting.

"I want to see her," he said. "All of her. Show me our girl, Joseph."

Joseph's hold on me shifted, and he guided me down onto my back. As soon as he broke our kiss, my thoughts became a little more rational. If I wasn't dreaming, then I had to stop this. I had to stop *them*. I couldn't betray Joseph. Not again.

I propped up on my elbows, bracing myself to scoot away.

Marco's hands closed around my shoulders at the same time as Joseph's hands gripped my bare thighs, and they both pushed me back down.

A part of my mind told me to struggle, to do what was right. But my body went oddly supple, my muscles melting under their firm touch. My eyes practically rolled back in my head as pleasure rushed through me. My heart pounded in my chest, and my pussy wept with my arousal. I'd never imagined it was possible to be this turned on. I ached deep inside, craving more.

"Relax, princess," Marco cooed. "Let Joseph make you feel good. I want him to show me what you like."

"Hold her wrists," Joseph told him. "She loves that."

Marco chuckled. "Of course she does."

They were talking about me, discussing me. It should have been insulting, but their rapt attention made me squirm. They stared down at me like I was the most fascinating thing they'd ever seen. Two sets of intense eyes studied me: depthless black and stunning blue.

Marco released my shoulders so he could capture my wrists. His long fingers encircled them fully, and he drew my arms over my head. He squeezed slightly as he pinned my hands against the pillow, reinforcing his control over me.

A strange, feral sound eased up my throat, and a wicked smile split his features.

Joseph's hands fisted in the silky nightgown, and he ripped the flimsy material down the middle with one jerk of his powerful arms. It wasn't the first time he'd stripped me like this, but it was different this time. I felt like he was stripping away all my defenses and exposing my soul.

"I liked that one," Marco commented. "The pink looks very sweet on her."

"I'll buy her another one. I'll buy her ten more."

His fingers teased beneath the torn fabric, slowly parting it to expose my body.

"I..." I struggled to formulate a protest. "I can't do this. I shouldn't. Joseph, I—"

"Hush, angel," he said gently. He began to stroke my skin in the reverent way that drove me wild. "I want this. Marco wants this. And I think you do too. If you don't want it, just say *stop*, and we'll stop. Do you want us to stop?"

I bit my lip and shook my head, too much of a coward to admit aloud that I didn't want them to stop. I wanted Joseph to keep caressing me. I wanted Marco to keep holding me down. I wanted them both to keep admiring me like I was the most breathtaking thing they'd ever seen.

"No more teasing, Joseph," Marco said gruffly. "I need to see her."

Joseph obliged him, easing the ruined nightgown aside so the silky fabric pooled at my sides. I heard Marco's sharp intake of breath, and I watched as his thick fingers neared my breasts. My skin tingled when he trailed his fingertips over the soft swells, and I arched toward his touch.

"You're even prettier than I imagined, princess," he told me, his voice soft with awe. His touch swirled around my nipples, and they pebbled to throbbing peaks. "Do you want Joseph to suck on your sweet little nipples?"

"Yes," I whined, hardly able to believe that this was happening, that I was allowing them to do this to me.

"Yes, *Daddy*," he corrected me.

My cheeks flamed red hot at the word, and I shot a shy glance at Joseph. Surely, he wouldn't want me to say that? Surely, he would think it was weird?

His pale gaze fixed firmly on mine. "Go on," he said. "Be a good girl for Marco."

A small whimper eased up my throat, and I shivered as a fresh wave of lust rolled over me. I was caught between them. What they were asking of me was dirty and wrong, but they were handling me carefully, as though they cherished me.

"Do you want Joseph to suck on your nipples, little girl?" Marco prompted, his voice dropping impossibly deeper.

"Yes, Daddy," I whispered.

Marco hummed his approval, and he leaned closer to me. "You make me very happy, babygirl," he said, just before his lips crashed down on mine. At the same time, Joseph's hot tongue flicked my nipple.

I cried out against Marco, and his tongue surged inside my mouth. He kissed me roughly, hungrily. Joseph began to tease and torment my breasts. He'd grazed them with his teeth a few times before, but he was being harsher with my body this time, more demanding. He nipped at the tight buds, sending sizzling lines of pleasure straight from my breasts to my clit. I rocked my hips up, mindlessly seeking stimulation. Marco's ruthless kiss was making me delirious, depriving me of oxygen and making my head spin.

When he finally broke contact, I gasped in a desperate breath, only to let it out on a harsh cry as Joseph bit my nipple. He released it immediately, soothing away the pain with his tongue. My lashes fluttered as pleasure washed through me. I trembled in Marco's hold, and I continued to roll my hips into the air, seeking Joseph's attention where I needed it most.

"Lick her pussy, Joseph," Marco ordered. "I know she tastes like fucking heaven, but I'll let you do it this time."

This time? I could hardly wrap my head around this happening once. Marco implied we'd do this again. But I couldn't contemplate his words. All thought was blown from my mind when Joseph settled between my thighs and touched his tongue to my clit.

Stars burst across my vision, and Marco caught my sharp scream in his mouth when his lips descended on mine again. He took me more gently, taking his time to taste and explore. Even though he wasn't as rough with me, I felt even more thoroughly conquered.

I wriggled beneath him and whined against his tongue as Joseph's mouth tormented my pussy. He teased around my clit and lapped at the wetness seeping from my core, but he didn't touch me firmly enough to push me over the edge. He was driving me higher and higher with each swipe of his tongue, but it wasn't quite enough.

"You want to come, don't you, princess?" Marco murmured against my lips.

I nodded and made a wordless sound of longing when Joseph's tongue swirled around my clit again.

"Don't let her come, Joseph," he warned. "Play with her ass first."

My eyes flew wide, and I shook my head. He couldn't. I couldn't let him do that. It was too...

I gasped when his fingertip dipped into my wet arousal before trailing farther back.

"Joseph hasn't touched your tight little asshole,

has he, babygirl?" Marco asked, but he didn't wait for me to answer. My response was plain on my face. "He's been holding back with you. Not anymore. You can handle us. You can take what we need to do to you."

Joseph's finger brushed across my puckered bud, and I tensed.

Marco kept his hold on my wrists with one hand and brushed my hair away from my sweat-damped brow with the other. "Let Joseph in, princess. He's going to make you feel so good."

Joseph's mouth came down on my clit again, and his tongue flicked over the tight bud. Pleasure surged through me, and I relaxed for a moment. He pressed his advantage, and the tip of his finger penetrated me.

I gasped and squirmed, but he didn't withdraw. It felt weird and invasive and...

"Oh!" I gasped as his tongue drove deep inside my pussy. His finger slipped in to the first knuckle, the lubrication of my own arousal easing his progress.

I clenched around him, trying to push him out. The sensation of my muscles rippling around his immovable finger lit up sensitive nerve endings I'd never imagined I possessed.

Joseph groaned against me. "She just gushed all over my tongue," he told Marco.

Marco bit out a curse. His hand fisted in my hair, tipping my head back so he could capture me in his burning gaze.

"You are so perfect, Ashlyn." He kept me fixed in his onyx stare, but he addressed Joseph. "Let her come. She's earned it."

Joseph's tongue parted my swollen folds again, and he brought his thumb down on my clit. He began rubbing in firm, rhythmic circles, and he pressed his forefinger deeper into my ass.

I shattered on a scream, and my eyes closed as bliss assailed me. Marco's fingers tightened in my hair, commanding my attention.

"No," he growled. "Look at me. Look at Daddy while you come."

My eyes locked on his, and ecstasy pulsed through me as my inner muscles contracted around Joseph's invasive finger. Marco watched me with a twisted smile as my entire body convulsed with pleasure.

Joseph continued to stimulate me, gently pumping his finger in and out of my ass as my body finally surrendered to the taboo intrusion. My sex grew sensitive, the pleasure too overwhelming to bear any more. I whimpered and tried to move away from his mouth and hands, but he didn't stop until Marco told him to.

"Enough, Joseph. You can play with her more next time."

Joseph finally withdrew from me and stepped away. Marco laid down beside me and pulled me into his arms, easing the ruined nightgown from my body. I heard water running in the bathroom, and then Joseph returned a minute later. He climbed onto the bed on my other side.

"You did so well, angel," he praised, stroking my back as Marco petted my hair. I was surrounded by their heat, their strength.

Everything started to seem surreal again, and I was so sleepy. I yawned, and Marco chuckled. He kissed my forehead.

"Go to sleep, princess. We can talk about everything in the morning."

I didn't want to talk about anything. I didn't want to think about anything. I just wanted to stay here, cocooned in bliss and their body heat.

So, I closed my eyes and obeyed Marco, falling into sleep.

Chapter Six
ASHLYN

I woke up, alone and cold. I felt the sheets beside me, searching for Joseph's warmth.

Joseph. He hadn't been the only one to cuddle me while I fell asleep.

I became aware of the sheets caressing my bare body.

I was naked. Joseph had ripped off my nightgown while Marco held me down. They...

My stomach did a funny flip.

Wrong. So dirty and wrong.

How could Joseph share me with his friend like that? Just yesterday, I'd almost been ready to confess my love for him. He must think of me as nothing more than a slut. Otherwise, he never would have allowed Marco to touch me like that. Once he learned that I'd cheated with his best friend, he must have decided I was a whore.

My body burned at the memory of their hands on me, and I recognized that the heat wasn't entirely the result of shame. My sex throbbed, and my nipples peaked against the cool sheets. I buried my face in the pillow, biting my lip against the sensation.

Maybe I *was* a slut. I must be, to come so hard while two men held me down. Joseph had fingered my virgin ass, and I'd come all over his face.

This isn't me. This is crazy. I'm acting crazy.

Ever since Marco had brought me to his mansion, I'd become more of a sexual being with each passing day. I'd fallen into Joseph's arms, willingly abandoning my life at Harvard. I'd traded my responsibilities for the pleasure of his touch.

Within the space of a few weeks, I'd become such a whore that I'd allowed two men to use me. I'd allowed Marco to *spank* me. I'd called him *Daddy*, and it had gotten me hot.

It was weird and taboo and *wrong*.

Get out. I had to get out before I lost myself completely. I'd allowed myself to forget that Marco had kidnapped me, that I was being held here against my wishes. All I'd wanted was to go back to Cambridge with Joseph, but I'd become docile and warped in my time on this estate.

Now, he'd never love me. I'd lost his respect and the respect of everyone else in my life: my professors, my father.

Joseph wasn't here this morning, holding me and calling me his *angel*. I'd never be his angel again. I was dirty now, damaged goods.

I threw the covers back and hastily found some clothes to cover my nakedness. I jerked on the yoga pants and camisole. I wished I had a coat to keep me warm once I ran outside, but I'd be in the warmth of Marco's BMW soon enough.

The men had left me alone. The bedroom door was open. They hadn't bothered to lock their compliant captive in her cage.

I knew if I could just make it to the garage, I could retrieve Marco's keys where he kept them hanging in a neat row. Once I got into the BMW, I could get off the estate. I'd ram my way through the gates if I had to.

I picked up my flats, deciding to carry them so I could walk across the marble floor of the foyer without making any noise. I wasn't sure where Marco and Joseph were, but at least one of them would be in the house. Probably Joseph. Marco often left to go into the city to deal with his *business*.

How could I have forgotten what that business

was? Marco and Joseph were criminals, and last night, they'd revealed their true, depraved nature.

I tiptoed down the stairs on bare feet. As I descended, I could make out the rumble of their voices emanating from the kitchen.

They were both here.

My heart hammered against my ribcage as adrenaline surged. If they caught me, I'd be helpless in their strong arms. I wouldn't be able to escape them.

I got to the front door and turned the knob slowly. The latch slid back silently.

I didn't dare close the door behind me in case it made noise, so I left it cracked.

I shivered as soon as the chilled autumn air hit my exposed skin, but I broke into a run. My feet sank into the grass as I tore around the side of the house, making my way toward the garage.

Luck was with me, because I didn't hear sounds of pursuit. I reached the garage without incident, and I slipped in the side door. I found the BMW keys on their designated peg, in their neatly organized place.

I rushed to the car and cranked the engine to life. The garage door seemed to take an eternity to lift open, but eventually, there was enough space for me to hit the gas. In my haste to get away, the tires squealed against the asphalt, but I was already in the safety of the car. I sped around the house and headed for the long driveway that led out of the estate.

The front door to the house burst open, revealing Joseph and Marco. Their shouts followed me down the driveway, and I saw them running in the rearview mirror. They weren't running after me. That would be futile. They were headed toward the garage, likely to get their own vehicle to pursue me.

I pressed my foot down on the gas pedal, increasing my speed.

In a matter of minutes, the gates appeared before me. They weren't pretty, wrought iron gates; they were solid steel.

My heart jumped into my throat, but I didn't have a choice.

I screamed as I barreled toward the barrier between me and freedom. I caught sight of the red Porsche in my rearview, and I firmed my resolve.

A shockwave hit my body when the car smashed into the gates. The hood of the car crumpled, and the airbag deployed. Pain burst through my head just before the world flickered around me.

The car door was wrenched open, and Joseph's panicked voice penetrated my pained haze as he freed me from my seatbelt.

"Ashlyn," he rasped. "You're okay. You're okay." He repeated it several times, sounding as though he was trying to convince himself as much as reassure me.

His arms closed around me, and he lifted me up. The world spun as he moved my body, and I groaned when pain spiked through my head.

"Shit, shit." That was Marco's voice. "I'm calling a doctor. Get her back to the house."

Something warm and wet trickled down my cheek, and my forehead stung.

I closed my eyes against the spinning world, falling into darkness.

∽

Everything was soft and warm. I was floating.

"Give her more," Marco demanded. "She's hurt."

"She'll be fine," a strange man's voice said. "I can't give her any more painkillers. She'll have a headache when she wakes up, but she's okay."

I hummed my contentment, happy to continue floating.

I recognized the feel of both their hands gripping mine; Joseph on my right, Marco on my left.

Reassured, I sank into the warmth.

∽

My throat was dry, and my head ached. I stirred with a groan.

"Here. Drink this."

I kept my eyes closed, but I knew it was Marco who propped me up and Joseph who held the glass to my lips. I gratefully gulped down the water.

"Open your mouth," Joseph commanded when he pulled the glass away.

I complied with that order, too.

Something small and round dropped onto my tongue, and the glass returned to my lips.

"Swallow it. You'll feel better soon."

I did as I was told, swallowing down the pill.

Marco was still holding me up, and his other hand was wrapped around mine. He squeezed gently, and I finally opened my eyes to look at him.

His gaze was dark, the fine lines on his face drawn with concern. His thumb traced little circular patterns on my palm.

"You scared me, babygirl."

"What were you thinking?" Joseph demanded, his cutting voice making my head throb.

I winced, and he softened his tone. He set the now-empty glass aside and took my other hand in his. "Why did you do that, angel?"

My mind was still foggy. "You think I'm a slut."

My words were thick on my heavy tongue. "I had to get away."

"Of course I don't think you're a slut. You're perfect: our sweet girl. You got yourself hurt."

"It was wrong," I slurred. "You... Both of you..." I couldn't quite focus on why I should protest. My mind was growing foggier, my body heavier.

"Yes," Marco said firmly. "Both of us. We care about you. We don't want anything to happen to you. Go back to sleep, princess. We'll be here when you wake up."

He eased me down onto the bed, and I drifted off without a thought.

Chapter Seven
MARCO

It took a couple days before Joseph and I eased off on feeding Ashlyn painkillers. Neither of us could bear to see her in pain, and we only woke her for meals and to see to her essential needs before we dosed her again.

She wasn't hurt. Not really. She had a small cut on her forehead. I knew how freely even benign head wounds could bleed, but the sight of crimson blood trailing down her pale cheek had made panic rip through my system.

If we hadn't been ensuring her comfort, her entire body would've ached from the whiplash. Thank fuck the BMW's safety features had protected her. The doctor we'd called to the house had promised she'd be fine after a few days of rest.

My car was totaled, but I didn't give a fuck about

that. I'd been more concerned about the structural integrity of the gates. Now that I'd almost lost Ashlyn, I was more fiercely protective than ever. I couldn't allow our enemies the opportunity to slip into our safe haven. I couldn't let them get to her.

They'd proven they were watching the estate when Ricky had threatened her at the restaurant. So, I'd paid a small fortune to get the gates repaired on the same day she'd smashed into them. The damage to the sturdy structure had been minimal, but I wasn't taking any chances.

Our fortress was secure again, and no one would get in.

Or out.

If Ashlyn thought she could leave us, she was mistaken.

"This is our fault, you know," Joseph told me as I paced back and forth across the bedroom. Ashlyn was taking a shower, her head finally clearing from the drugs. We were waiting for her to come out.

I didn't understand how Joseph could so calmly sit on the bed. Anxious energy flooded my system. I had to keep moving, or I'd crawl out of my skin.

"She tried to run away," I growled. "She got herself hurt. She has a severe punishment coming for that."

"Yes," he agreed. "But we need to talk to her first.

We scared her, Marco. We should've explained more before we played with her together."

"That wasn't *play*, and you know it," I snapped. We'd never shared such an intense connection with a woman, and neither of us had even fucked her.

"I know. But she doesn't understand. She said she's worried I think she's a slut." His lips thinned and his fists clenched, his calm demeanor slipping.

I ground my teeth at the word. My innocent little princess was far from a slut. She might submit to our depraved games, but we worshipped her.

We had to make her understand.

Then, I could punish her. My body practically vibrated with the need to discipline her, to show her that I'd never allow her to put herself in danger again. She was my responsibility, and I'd protect her from anything, even herself.

After what felt like an hour, Ashlyn finally emerged from the bathroom. Her hair was damp, her cheeks pink from the heat of the shower. She'd dressed in her camisole and yoga pants instead of one of the sexy nightgowns Joseph had bought for her.

I didn't like it, even if I could see her nipples through the thin top. She'd chosen this outfit as a barrier between us, a denial of the sexual chemistry we shared. If I could have my way, she'd be naked right now, crying out at the sting of my discipline while she squirmed over Joseph's lap.

I took a deep breath. There would be plenty of time for that after we explained everything to her. I couldn't stand the idea that she thought of herself as a slut. We hadn't meant to demean her, and judging by her ecstatic reaction to us when we both held her, I hadn't been prepared for her emotional backlash. She'd allowed us to cuddle her between us after her explosive orgasm, so sweet and trusting as she fell asleep in our arms. I'd assumed she'd wake up smiling in the morning, and we could discuss everything over breakfast.

We never should have left her alone in bed. She'd probably thought we'd abandoned her.

That had been our mistake. I intended to rectify it right now.

"Come sit with me, angel." Joseph patted the mattress beside him. "We need to talk."

She hesitated, shooting me a shy glance.

"All of us," Joseph added more sternly.

She crossed the room slowly, but she sat beside him on the bed. I wanted to join them, to wrap my arm around her and hold her close.

But I couldn't touch her. Not until I was sure she'd welcome me. If she cringed away from me now, it would tear me apart. I might damage things beyond repair if I pushed too hard. She had to be willing. She might be our captive, but I would never do anything to harm her or cause her distress.

Joseph wasn't as hesitant as I was. He reached out and took her hand in his. She stiffened, but she didn't pull away.

She still trusted him. She still cared for him.

Something ached deep in my chest, but I ignored it.

"You shouldn't have run from us," Joseph told her, his voice gentle despite the rebuke. "You got yourself hurt. And if you had left the estate, our enemies could've gotten their hands on you. We won't allow that to happen."

"I can't stay here," she whispered, pained. "I just want to go back to school. I..." Her voice hitched. "I don't want to be here with you."

I could hear the lie in her strained tone, but I didn't call her on it. We needed to handle this with finesse, so I'd let Joseph take the lead. He'd always been smoother than I was. I couldn't help being blunt and saying exactly what I thought. If I opened my mouth, I'd warn her about the dangers she faced without us to guard her. That wasn't what she needed to hear right now.

"You can't go back, angel," Joseph said, soothing. "It's too dangerous."

She stared at him, imploring. "I can't stay here with you. You think... You don't respect me. I never should've agreed to stay away from school. No one respects me anymore. I'm just a...a slut."

"I never want to hear you say that word again," I growled, unable to hold back.

She glanced my way, then quickly dropped her eyes.

"Marco's right," Joseph said firmly. "Don't use that word. You are not a slut. I respect you. Marco respects you. We care about you, Ashlyn. We want to be with you. Both of us."

Her brow furrowed. "But that...that's wrong. I'm supposed to be with you, Joseph."

I bit the inside of my cheek hard enough that coppery blood spilled onto my tongue.

"But you want to be with Marco, too," he told her. "It's okay. We want it to be this way. This is how it should be. You were made for us, angel. Both of us."

"I don't understand," she murmured, but her cheeks were pink with something other than shame.

"Marco and I like to share. We've always been this way."

I remembered clearly how we'd fallen into this

dynamic. Joseph and I had always shared a tight bond. I'd taken on the role of his protector when he was a scrawny kid, and I'd become responsible for him. He meant more to me than a brother, but I thought of him with similar affection I might feel for a younger sibling.

I was five years older, and I'd been with my share of women by the time Joseph was ready to lose his virginity. He'd opened up to me about how nervous he was. He'd asked me for guidance. So, I'd provided it. In person.

Telling him how to touch that woman to get her off had been the hottest experience of my life. It hadn't taken long for us to start sharing in more extreme ways. Over time, Joseph had developed his tastes in kinky toys, but I'd always been the one who was ultimately in charge.

We might not engage with each other sexually, but Joseph was still mine. Mine to guide and protect. I'd always had his back, and it had killed me when he'd disappeared. During his time hiding out in Cambridge, I'd worried he was dead.

That still stung a little, as did Ashlyn's distance from me. She thought she was supposed to belong to Joseph because she'd been with him first. Her insistence that she should share a relationship only with him was a mark of her loyalty, not a rejection of me. I admired her for that loyalty. Fuck, I wanted her fierce loyalty for myself. For me and Joseph.

We had to make her understand what we wanted from her. What we needed.

"My feelings about you haven't changed because you kissed Marco," Joseph told her. "I'm happy you want to be with him too. Don't you care for him?"

"I..." She bit her lip against the admission. She still thought it was wrong, a betrayal to Joseph.

"Tell us the truth," he prompted in a deeper tone that made her shiver.

"Yes," she breathed.

He trailed his fingers through her hair, and she leaned into his touch.

"Look at Marco, and tell him how you feel."

Her sapphire eyes met mine. They were still dark with confusion, but she uttered the words that made my heart squeeze.

"I care about you, Marco. I thought I was scared of you, but I'm not. Not really."

I nodded. "So, you understand? We both need you, Ashlyn. We'll never get jealous or fight over you. We're supposed to be together. The three of us."

"Don't you want that, angel?" Joseph asked, coaxing.

She nodded, still too shy to give voice to her secret longings.

"I need to hear you say it," I told her. "Tell us you want us."

She licked her lips. "I want you," she whispered. "Both of you."

I finally allowed myself to close the distance between us. I wrapped my hand around her nape and bent down to crush my lips against hers. She was soft under my mouth, pliant. She shuddered and opened for me, welcoming me. I kissed her until she sagged into Joseph's waiting arms.

When she was trembling and gasping for breath, I finally released her.

"I think it's time to punish our naughty girl," I told Joseph.

"Past time," he agreed.

"What are you—" Before she could finish her question, Joseph had her over his lap.

She tried to kick out, flailing in surprise more than struggling to be free. Joseph caught her wrists and pinned them at the small of her back before settling his other arm around the backs of her knees, effectively ending her struggles.

"What are you doing?" she panted.

I stepped in front of her so she could watch me unbuckle my belt. I took it off slowly, allowing the leather to whisper against my jeans.

Her wide eyes fixed on my movements, and she

licked her lips. My cock throbbed, but now wasn't the time to explore the silky heat of her mouth.

"You shouldn't have tried to run away, princess," I told her. "You put yourself in danger. You were hurt. We can't allow that kind of behavior."

I doubled the belt over and touched the leather beneath her chin, lifting her face so she had no choice but to stare up into my eyes.

"We're going to punish you because we care about you. We care enough to correct your rash behavior. You want that, don't you?"

"I don't want you to hurt me," she said, her voice small.

"This is going to sting, babygirl." I wouldn't lie to her. "You'll feel the heat of our discipline. I'm not going to beat you, but I am going to teach you a lesson."

Joseph peeled her pants down her thighs, exposing her pert ass. He dipped two fingers between her legs, testing her pussy.

"You're wet, angel," he told her, his voice husky with his own lust. "You want Marco to punish you while I hold you down."

"But why?" she asked, her eyes tight with confusion. "I don't understand why I'm like this. It's wrong."

"It's not wrong," I countered firmly, increasing the

pressure of the belt beneath her chin to keep her attention on me. "There's nothing wrong about the connection we share. I'm going to give you five lashes for trying to run away from us. I think you're ready for that. If you're not, say the word now, and everything will stop."

She stared up at me, and I watched her emotions flicker over her lovely face: doubt, embarrassment, longing.

She was ready.

"Okay, babygirl. Take a deep breath."

She obeyed, and I withdrew the belt from her chin. I laid the leather flat on her exposed ass, letting her feel its cool caress. Joseph took a few more seconds to stroke her pussy, making her squirm.

Our eyes met in silent communication, and Joseph nodded his agreement that she was prepared. He moved his hand out of my way and braced his arm behind her knees again. She was trapped, locked safely in place for my discipline. Joseph wouldn't let her flinch or wiggle away, and I didn't have to worry about any of my blows landing in the wrong place.

I let the first lick fall, and the *pop* of the leather against her skin mingled with her sharp cry. A bright red line bloomed across her bottom, contrasting with her creamy flesh.

"That hurt," she gasped out, her voice catching.

"It's supposed to hurt, princess. You were a naughty girl, and you have to learn your lesson. Four more."

I let the second hit land, and she squealed. She jerked in Joseph's arms, but he held her fast. I lashed her a third time, putting a little more force behind the belt. She didn't make any sound at all for a second, then a long wail left her chest.

"Just two more," I told her smoothly, reassuring her. "You can cry if you need to."

A harsh sob made her small body shudder. The sight of her tears didn't upset me. She needed this. She needed the correction, the attention, the affection. Because even though I was causing her a little pain, I was taking her in hand to protect her.

I landed the last two lashes in quick succession, spreading out the sting. She shrieked, and her back arched as her muscles tensed for a moment. Then, she went limp against Joseph, her head dropping forward as her tears dripped down onto the sheets.

I let my belt fall from my fingers and held out my arms. Joseph passed her to me, and I cradled her against my chest as I settled down on the edge of the bed. I cuddled her close and kissed the wetness on her cheeks. She didn't shudder or shy away from me. She tucked her face against my neck, and her fingers curled into my shirt.

Warmth expanded in my chest. I'd been right about her from the very beginning. Ashlyn might have given herself to Joseph a long time ago, but she was meant for me, too. She was mine. Ours.

Our sweet girl.

Chapter Eight
ASHLYN

"Why did Joseph have to leave?" I asked as I sat down at the kitchen island. I winced when my sore bottom settled onto the padded stool, but the discomfort was accompanied by a rush of heat between my legs.

I still didn't understand why I was like this, and I'd wanted to talk to both of them more. But after my tears had dried, Joseph regretfully told me he had to leave me with Marco for the day.

Just last week, the thought of being alone with Marco would've made me anxious. Now, he still made me a little nervous, but I craved more time with him. I wanted to understand him better. I wanted to understand what was happening between us better.

Us. The three of us. Joseph, Marco, and me.

I could still barely wrap my head around it. This was... Well, Marco had told me it wasn't *wrong*. But it was certainly unconventional, to say the least.

How could I have feelings for two men at the same time? And how could they possibly be okay with that?

Marco had promised that they wouldn't get jealous, that they wanted to be with me. At the same time.

The memory of their hands holding me down—Marco kissing me while Joseph licked my pussy and fingered my ass—made me flush, and not with shame.

I'd been a fool to try to run away without giving them the chance to explain. And even though my bottom smarted from Marco's belt, I felt more centered and at peace than I had since I'd arrived at his estate. I'd spent weeks skirting around Marco, hiding behind Joseph. I'd told myself he frightened me, but I was actually scared of the dark chemistry we shared.

I still didn't fully understand it, but that didn't change my feelings or the intensity of my sensual connection to both men.

"Joseph's father asked to meet with him," Marco answered my question as he made his way to the refrigerator. "They need to talk business."

"Oh." My heart sank a little. I couldn't help caring for both Joseph and Marco, but the reminder that Joseph had other responsibilities shattered the illusion of my happy little reality. No matter what he wanted for his life, he was still part of the criminal underworld. And so was Marco.

"What's wrong, babygirl?"

I blinked and focused on Marco again. I didn't want to bring up their violent lifestyle, not when I knew there was nothing they could do about it. At least, not right now. Joseph had made it clear that he wanted out, that he wanted to go back to Cambridge with me when the danger had passed. I hoped Marco would feel the same, because I didn't want to leave him behind, either.

"Why do you call me that?" I asked instead of telling him what was really bothering me.

"Because you're my girl, and I want to take care of you."

"Is that why..." I blushed, but I pressed on. "Is that why you want me to call you Daddy?"

He nodded. "Exactly. I don't just want you to be my girlfriend, Ashlyn. What I want is so much more than that: a deeper bond. I know this is new for you, but I want to show you what that means. I have a special day planned for us."

"What did you have in mind?" I fiddled with my fingernails, feeling suddenly nervous. So far, Marco had spanked me and whipped me with his belt. "Are you going to punish me again? Because I'm sorry for trying to run away. I really am."

"I know you are, princess. And no, I'm not going to punish you again. Not unless you decide to be very naughty. I know your bottom is sore right now, and I don't want to discipline you again so soon. What I do want is to take care of you, in the way I need to. I want you to let me."

"But what does that mean?" I liked the idea of Marco taking care of me—his affection for me was like nothing I'd ever known. Joseph had been obsessed with me from the very beginning of our relationship. He'd wanted me to belong to him, to submit to him. I understood that now.

But Marco wanted something different from me. Something dark and strange. Something that made me tremble, even as my entire body heated for him.

"I'm your Daddy. I'll show you what it means. All you need to do is be a good girl and do as you're told."

"What if I don't want to do what I'm told?"

He gave me a lopsided grin that made my heart melt. How had it taken me so long to appreciate how handsome he was? Joseph might be gorgeous, but Marco possessed his own dark beauty.

"You can pout all you want, princess. It's adorable, but it won't get you anywhere with me. You'll do as you're told, because it'll make me happy. And you want to make Daddy happy, don't you?"

I mulled that over. It was weird, unlike anything I'd ever heard of.

But of course I wanted Marco to be happy. I craved his pleasure, his smile.

"Yes," I agreed. "I want you to be happy, Marco."

"*Daddy*," he corrected me.

My cheeks flamed, but the words left my lips without a second thought. "I want you to be happy, Daddy."

His brilliant grin knocked the air from my chest. "That's my sweet girl."

I returned his smile, giddy excitement flooding my system. I liked when he spoke to me with such warm approval.

Marco started gathering what he needed from the fridge to make lunch.

"You don't have to make all my meals." I'd let him make every meal for me since I'd arrived. I hadn't lifted a finger to help. And while I wasn't much of a cook, I suddenly felt guilty for taking Marco for granted.

He shot me a warning look. "I want to, and don't let me hear you say another word about it. I told you: I'm going to take care of you today. Let me."

"Okay." I felt a little useless, sitting here while he worked. So, I passed the short span of time by watching his bulky muscles flex and shift as he moved. His tight black shirt did little to hide his physique, and his dark jeans hugged his ass perfectly.

I was practically drooling by the time he sat down beside me, placing a single plate between us. The sandwich was stuffed with enough pastrami for two people, and he'd provided far more hummus and carrot sticks than I could eat by myself.

"Where's yours?" I asked, puzzled.

"This is for both of us."

"Oh." I still didn't understand why we were sharing off one plate, but he'd cut the sandwich down the middle, so I supposed there was enough food for both of us.

I reached for my half, but he caught my wrist and directed my hand back to my lap. He picked up a carrot stick and dipped it in the hummus before lifting it to my mouth.

"What are you doing?" I asked.

"Taking care of you. Open up, babygirl."

"I can feed myself."

"Of course you can. But I want to feed you today.

Now, be a good girl for Daddy and eat your vegetables."

This was weird. It made me uncomfortable and hot and tingly.

My lips parted, and the salty hummus touched my tongue. The carrot crunched beneath my teeth, sweet mingling with salt.

Marco's smile hit me square in the chest. I'd never seen him like this: proud and pleased in a way I couldn't fully comprehend.

Even though I couldn't quite wrap my head around it, I basked in his pleasure. If allowing him to feed me felt this good, why fight it?

Marco watched me intently as I ate every bite he brought to my lips, his eyes darkening and his lids growing heavy as I complied. He even held my glass of water to my lips, insisting that I drink intermittently. He needed me to do as he told me. I could see it in the way his lips curved with satisfaction when I obeyed.

His pleasure was catching. By the time I finished my lunch, my body felt strangely light, and I was grinning like a fool. I didn't have a care or worry in my head, because Marco was taking care of me.

He held my hand while he ate his own share of our meal, as though he couldn't bear to break contact with me.

I didn't want him to, either.

When he polished off the last of the food, he cleaned up the plate and came back to me. He held out his hand, waiting for me to wrap my fingers around his. I did so without hesitation, and he led me to the media room.

Well, he called it the *media room*. It was more like an in-home theater. The massive screen took up one wall, and the plush sectional couch could have easily seated ten people.

He sat in one corner of the couch, propping back against it while he stretched his legs out in front of him. I moved to sit beside him, but he shifted my body with his sure, strong hands. When he was finished moving me into position, I laid on my side, stretched out beside him with my head resting on his thighs.

He stroked my hair with one hand and picked up the remote with the other.

Tears filled my eyes when the movie started. Nostalgia and affection for Marco swelled.

The Last Unicorn.

"You remembered," I murmured.

"Of course I did. Now hush, and watch the movie."

He continued stroking my hair, his fingers playing through the silken strands in a hypnotic rhythm. As I sank into relaxation, he rubbed my scalp and my nape in a light massage. I melted against him, humming in contentment as the familiar story played out on the screen.

By the time the credits rolled, I felt even lighter than I had after lunch. I'd thought my dynamic with Marco was complicated, but being with him like this was so simple. Easy. I didn't have to stress or make any hard decisions. I didn't have to worry about my responsibilities or what anyone expected of me.

All that mattered was what Marco expected of me, and that was to be good for him and let him take care of me.

I rolled onto my back and looked up at him. He practically radiated contentment, and he continued stroking me.

"Why am I like this?" I asked him. "I mean, I like what we're doing. But it's not normal, is it?" I wasn't concerned about it anymore. I was curious.

"Does it matter if it's normal? Does it matter what other people think, if this makes both of us happy?"

"I guess not. I still don't understand, though."

His hand stilled in my hair for a moment. "Tell me about your relationship with your parents."

I flinched; the question punctured my happy little bubble.

He resumed petting me. "We don't have to talk about this now, but if you want to understand, it would help if I knew more about your upbringing."

"There's not much to talk about," I hedged.

A small frown tugged at his lips. "Don't hide from me," he warned. "I know your father never responded to your email about taking time off from college. I know you didn't message your mother at all. Are you estranged from your parents?"

I tried to turn my face away, but his fingers tightened in my hair, trapping me beneath his incisive gaze.

"My dad loves me." Even I could hear how defensive I sounded. "He just has high expectations. He wants me to succeed."

"He puts a lot of pressure on you," Marco read the truth in my words. "You're obviously intelligent and hardworking. You wouldn't have been accepted at Harvard, otherwise. Does your father tell you he's proud of you?"

"No," I whispered. "Not really." It was expected that I would work hard and do well, so there was no need for positive reinforcement when I succeeded. There was only a need for censure when I failed.

"And what about your mother?"

"We don't really talk."

"Why not?" he pressed, not willing to let me stop there.

My eyes stung. "Well, my parents divorced when I was eight. My mother moved to Chicago for her career, and she decided it was best for me to stay with Dad. She works crazy hours." A lump formed in my throat, but I continued. "Then, she met someone new. She got remarried and started a new family in Chicago. She forgot about me in Savannah."

All I'd wanted for as long as I could remember was to have a family of my own. I dreamed about getting married and having babies. I longed to have people in my life I could love unconditionally. People who would love me in return.

I didn't dare voice that dream aloud to my father or my friends. It was expected that I would go to a prestigious college and get more than my MRS. Degree. My father would be appalled if he knew that I wanted to meet a man who would start a family with me.

Marco brushed a tear from my cheek. "You want someone to take care of you. Someone who's proud of you for who you are, not what they want you to be. And that's okay."

"Is it?" I asked desperately. "I've lived my whole life trying to impress my dad. He'd be so ashamed if he knew all I really want is to get married and have babies. All I want is to stay at home and raise my children."

"You don't have to worry about what your father thinks," he said firmly. "What he wants you to be doesn't matter. What matters is what will make you happy. This is your life, Ashlyn. Not his. If you never want to go back to school, that's okay. Know that whatever you choose, *I'll* be proud of you. I'll take care of you, no matter what."

My tears spilled over his fingers, falling faster than he could wipe them away. No one had ever told me they were proud of me, and certainly not unconditionally. It was why I didn't trust people easily; if I let myself be open and vulnerable for even a second, I might get hurt.

"I've always felt like I have to be perfect in everything I do, or my dad would be disappointed in me," I admitted.

"I think you're perfect. Just the way you are."

He lifted me up in his arms, holding me close while I cried cathartic tears. I'd never told anyone my deepest secrets before. I'd never trusted anyone like I was trusting Marco. Not even Joseph, even though I'd wanted to open up to him.

"Do you understand now, babygirl?" he asked when my tears subsided. "Does the way you feel about me make sense?"

"Yes," I said, my voice still thick from crying. "But what about you? Why do you like this?"

All I could see was my benefit from this dynamic. Marco took care of me, and I didn't have to do anything to earn his affection.

But what did he get out of taking on that responsibility?

His jaw firmed, but he continued to cuddle me close. "I need someone to take care of. I need to feel needed, necessary," he admitted. "I don't have a great relationship with my father, either. Joseph is my only family now."

"What about your mom?" I asked softly, almost afraid to push him.

His eyes shuttered. "She died when I was eleven."

Fresh tears flowed from my eyes, but this time, they were for him. "I'm so sorry." I could tell he wasn't ready to talk about her, about his pain. But it was enough that he'd shared his loss with me. I understood him better now. I understood why he wanted me in this particular, strange way.

He blinked and focused on me again, but his jaw was still clenched. "I have a surprise for you, princess."

He got to his feet, guiding me up with him.

"What is it?" I asked.

A ghost of his smile returned, but his eyes were still tight with worry. "I'll show you. Come on."

He led me through the massive house. I thought he must be taking me to the backyard, but instead, we entered the glass-walled conservatory.

At first, all I could see was the indoor garden. A large, rectangular patch of dirt was raised about four feet off the ground, walled in by patterned, pale blue tiles. A variety of floral bushes grew from the soil. I couldn't identify them, but the colorful blooms were pretty. I hadn't seen them up close before, because I'd never entered this space from inside the house. I'd only peered in at the pool when Joseph and I went for walks outside.

Marco led me around the indoor garden, and I sucked in a surprised gasp.

The pool.

It had been cleaned and filled, and the glowing blue water called to me, practically begging me to dive in.

I turned to him with a delighted giggle. "You fixed it for me," I exclaimed. "Thank you."

His lips curved in a smile, but tension lingered around his eyes. He seemed upset about something, and I didn't understand.

"What is it?" I asked, some of my joy deflating. "Why didn't you want me to go swimming?" I remembered the way he'd glared at Joseph when he'd asked Marco to get the pool serviced. I'd thought it was because Marco didn't care about my happiness, but now, he'd made it clear that wasn't the case.

He brushed a kiss against my forehead. "I like seeing you smile, princess. So, I changed my mind."

He hadn't really answered my question, but he didn't give me a chance to press him.

"Go on," he urged. "Get in."

"But I don't have a swimsuit."

A wicked grin chased away the last of his tension. "No, you don't. Strip."

I hesitated.

He leaned in close, his warm breath teasing over my neck. "Are you feeling shy, babygirl? Daddy's already seen you naked. I want to see you again. Be a good girl, and do as you're told."

My fingers trembled as I reached for the hem of my camisole, but I wasn't scared. Lust coursed through me, making me tingle all over. My entire body was aware of his nearness, his heat, his strength.

I wanted to make him happy. I wanted to be naked for him, so he could admire me. No one had ever looked at me the way Marco and Joseph did: like I was the most precious thing in their world.

They didn't think I was a slut they could use for their dirty games. They wanted to share me because they both revered me. It was heady knowledge, and my mind spun as I grew intoxicated by Marco's open admiration.

I tossed my shirt aside and shimmied out of my yoga pants. Since we'd been lounging around the house, I hadn't bothered to put on shoes, so I was fully bare for Marco in a matter of seconds. I no longer minded that Joseph hadn't provided me with underwear. I liked knowing that there was only a thin barrier between my body and my men's hands.

My men. Joseph and Marco. They were both mine. I could hardly believe it.

I reached for Marco's shirt, but he guided my hands away.

I glanced up into his dark eyes, puzzled. "Don't you want to get in with me?" I liked the idea of skinny-dipping with Marco. It seemed fun and silly and naughty.

"I'll be right here watching you, princess. Now, go on."

"Oh. Okay." I guessed it wasn't necessarily out of the ordinary. Not everyone liked to swim. And while I'd like to be more playful with Marco in the pool, I wouldn't at all mind swimming a few laps for the first time in months. I'd neglected my routine ever since I'd met Joseph at Harvard, and I longed to get back in the water.

I left Marco's side and stepped to the edge of the pool, at the deep end. I dived in, my outstretched arms slicing through the water with practiced ease. I swam the length of the pool, kicked off from the side, and completed my first lap. As I continued, my mind went quiet. I'd already been in a blissed-out state after my happy day with Marco, but now, I was even more relaxed.

After a while, I paused to take a few deep breaths, propping my arms on the tiled edge of the pool. I grinned up at Marco.

When my eyes met his, my smile melted.

His tension had returned, and his strong body practically vibrated. The hard planes of his face were harsher than ever, his jaw clenched so tight, I was sure he was grinding his teeth. He wasn't looking at me, but he was glaring at the water.

"You look like the water's going to attack me," I said, trying to lighten his mood. "You don't have to protect me from the pool."

He jerked his head in a sharp nod, but the taut lines of his face didn't ease. I studied him for a few seconds longer, trying to puzzle out his expression.

Anguish.

I pushed myself up out of the pool and closed the distance between us without a second thought. He didn't even glance down at the water sliding off my body; his eyes fixed on mine. They were dark with pain. I recognized it now.

When he'd glowered at Joseph at the restaurant, he hadn't been angry over Joseph asking him to fill the pool for me. He hadn't been annoyed at the idea of going out of his way to make the arrangements for me.

His anger masked his true emotions. He was scared. Hurt.

I lifted my hand to his face, touching my palm to his clenched jaw. "What's wrong?"

"I don't like pools," he said tersely. "They're not safe."

"I'm perfectly safe," I said calmly, trying to soothe him. "I've been swimming my entire life. And you're here, watching over me. Nothing bad is going to happen."

"Yes, I'm right here. And you're never allowed to use the pool unless I'm watching. Do you understand?"

"Do you not know how to swim?" I didn't understand why he was so upset.

"Of course I do. That's why I'm going to stay right here, in case you need me."

I stared up at him, trying to figure out what was going on in his head. He said he could swim, but he hadn't wanted to get in the pool with me. Now, he was talking like I might get hurt somehow if he wasn't here to guard me.

"Why are you so upset?" I finally asked the direct question, daring to push him.

His eyes flared with a flash of rage, but he didn't move a muscle. The anger wasn't directed at me.

"Because I wasn't always there," he almost shouted in my face, but I didn't flinch away. He needed to tell me something important, and I wouldn't show him how intimidated I was by his swinging mood. "My brother..." His voice broke, and he turned his face away.

I applied light pressure to his jaw, redirecting his gaze to mine. My stomach churned, and I wasn't at all sure I wanted to hear what was coming next.

But I needed to know. And whatever this secret was, Marco needed to share it with me. When I'd first met him, I'd thought there was something cold and dark about his soul. Now, I could see that darkness wasn't evil; it was a scar on his heart that he hid behind his cool exterior.

"Tell me," I whispered.

"My brother. Little Leo. He drowned. I should've been watching him, but I was too busy playing my own games. He was two years old. Then, my mother..." A shudder wracked his body. "She died three years later. Overdosed on alcohol and pills. I killed her, too."

"Marco," I said his name tremulously, my heart breaking for him. "You were just a little boy. You weren't responsible for what happened."

"Of course I was," he snapped. "I *am*. They're gone, and it's my fault. No wonder my father wants nothing to do with me."

"You deserve to be loved, Marco." The words came from deep in my soul. I wasn't ready to say *I love you* yet; it was too soon for that. What we shared was too new, but I needed him to know that no matter what had happened in his past, he deserved love.

"How can you say that?" he asked, strained. But longing lit his dark eyes.

"Because I care about you. Just the way you are," I mirrored his promise of unconditional affection he'd declared for me earlier.

I went up on my tiptoes and pressed my lips against his. He was stiff against me for a moment, but then his arms wrapped around me, pulling me close in a fierce embrace. He kissed me as though our connection was the only thing tethering him to sanity. And in a way, maybe it was. He'd told me he needed me.

I believed him.

He needed to take care of me, to take responsibility for my wellbeing. But he needed my devotion, my trust, in return.

I gave it to him, opening for him and allowing him to claim my mouth in harsh, hungry strokes of his tongue.

He stepped toward me, prompting me to move with him. My ass bumped into the cool tile wall that surrounded the garden.

He finally tore his mouth from mine, gasping for air.

"I need you, Ashlyn," he said, his voice rough with desire.

"Take me," I urged, pressing my body against his. I craved him as fiercely as he craved me. "I need you, too."

He groaned. "You make me so happy, babygirl. Daddy's going to fuck you now. Are you ready to take my cock like a good girl?"

"Yes, Daddy," I panted, losing myself in our strange new dynamic. "Please." My core ached, and my thighs were slick with more than water.

He bit out a curse and reached for his belt buckle, freeing himself from his jeans. I stared down at him. He was just as big as Joseph, his girth a little wider.

"Touch me," he ground out.

I stroked my fingers down his shaft, feeling him for the first time. He'd held me down and kissed me while Joseph licked my pussy, but I'd never been with Marco like this before. I wanted to learn every inch of him.

I wrapped my hand around his cock, stroking more boldly. He growled his appreciation, but he didn't give me much time to explore. His need was too intense, and so was mine.

He gripped my hips and turned me away from him. His big hand pressed between my shoulders, urging me to bend forward. I braced myself on my hands, my fingers digging into the cool garden soil as I thrust my ass back at him, offering myself.

His boot tapped my ankles, urging me to spread my legs wider for him. I complied, eager for him to join with me in the most intimate way possible.

"I don't have a condom," he ground out through gritted teeth. "But I'm clean. Are you on birth control?"

"Yes." I'd gotten the shot a few months ago. I'd never had unprotected sex before, but I longed to feel Marco inside me, with no barrier between us. "Please, Daddy." I arched my back, begging him with my body as well as my words.

"I like when you say my name, princess."

I felt his cockhead pressing at my slick entrance, and I pushed back, welcoming him. His fingers curled into my hips, holding me securely in place as he slowly entered me, inch by delicious inch. My body stretched to accommodate him, my arousal intense enough to ease his way. When his balls finally hit my pussy lips, I felt wonderfully full.

He stayed still inside me for several long seconds, until I started squirming against him.

His palm cracked against my ass, and his hand tangled in my hair, pressing my head down so my cheek rested on the soft soil. I was trapped, pinned in place and rebuked. My inner muscles contracted around him as I realized how much bigger he was, how strong and powerful. I was helpless in his hands, but I knew he'd never do anything to hurt me.

My muscles fluttered around him, and he hissed in a breath. I felt his cock jerk inside me, and I whined my need. He had to move within me, he had to…

"Oh!" I cried out as his cockhead dragged over my g-spot.

"You like Daddy's cock, babygirl?" he asked, the words rough with lust.

"Yes," I cried out. "More, please."

His grip on my hair shifted, tugging back. My head came up, his hold forcing me to arch against him. He drove back in, sinking impossibly deeper. I whimpered, and my fingers dug into the soil, scrambling for something to hold onto.

He started to take me faster, harder. With each thrust, pleasure lit up my system when he rubbed the sensitive spot at the front of my inner walls. The weight of his balls slapping against my lower lips only drove me higher.

"You're so tight, princess. Daddy's not going to last long."

Keeping his hold on my hair with one hand, his other reached around me to find my clit. He rubbed it in a firm, circular motion. I screamed and shattered, my pussy contracting around him as my orgasm claimed me with ruthless force.

He let out a feral roar, rutting into me as his cock pulsed with his own pleasure. His cum lashed into me, branding me deep inside. Primal chemicals mingled inside me, increasing my bliss.

I cried out and thrust back toward him mindlessly as we both rode out our ecstasy. His grip on my hair tightened, lighting up my scalp with little bites of pain that made my whole body tingle.

He thrust in one last time, driving deep with a long groan. His cum dripped down my thighs, and I shuddered as the aftershocks of my orgasm sizzled through me.

We both came down slowly, breathing hard. Finally, he pulled out and lifted me up in his arms, holding me against his chest as he claimed my mouth again.

I wrapped my arms around his neck and pulled him closer, reveling in our connection. It didn't feel strange anymore. It felt natural.

I'd thought this was wrong, but nothing had ever been more right.

Chapter Nine
ASHLYN

I sighed in contentment. After our intense sex in the conservatory, Marco had carried me upstairs and given me a bath. He'd washed and brushed my hair, telling me how sweet and beautiful I was in his deep, rumbling voice.

By the time Joseph returned home, I was completely relaxed, cuddled against Marco on the couch while we watched *Arrested Development*. Marco seemed to favor comedies, whereas Joseph enjoyed serialized dramas. I liked both, but I enjoyed snuggling up to them on the couch more than I cared about the show.

I beamed at Joseph when he joined us in the media room. He took one look at me cuddled in Marco's arms and grinned.

"Did you have a good day, then, angel?" he asked, closing the distance between us. He sat on my other side, wrapping his arm around me and pressing a quick kiss against my lips.

"Wonderful, thanks," I told him with genuine enthusiasm. "I'm glad you're back."

I'd loved my special day with Marco, but I'd missed Joseph. The way I needed him was different, but no less intense than the way I craved Marco. They both wanted to cherish me, in their own way. I could see that now. Marco needed my pure devotion, and Joseph needed my willing submission.

Marco's drawing popped into my mind for the first time in several days. The image of Joseph looming behind me, binding me with rope, made my sex heat and my cheeks flush.

One corner of Joseph's mouth tugged up in the crooked, knowing smile that made my heart melt.

"What are you thinking about, angel?"

"Marco's drawing," I answered honestly. There was no embarrassment anymore. I wasn't ashamed of my arousal in response to the image. I couldn't be ashamed of my attraction to Joseph and Marco. "The one of you tying me up," I clarified. "Is that something..." I swallowed, my throat suddenly dry. "Is that something you want?"

His clear blue eyes regarded me earnestly. "Only if it's something you want."

Marco brushed my hair back from my cheek. "Joseph likes his toys," he told me. "But we won't do anything that you don't like."

I shifted in my seat. "I don't know if I don't like it. I haven't been able to stop thinking about it."

"I told you," Marco said to Joseph.

"Yes, you did." Joseph took my hand in his, keeping his focus on me. "I thought those drawings scared you. I didn't want to push you. But yes, that is something I want."

"It's something you need," Marco clarified.

I kept my eyes on Joseph's. "What do you mean?" I understood Marco's needs now, but I still didn't fully grasp why Joseph enjoyed dominating me. I'd seen the dark pleasure in his eyes when he overpowered me. I wanted to understand him, the way I now understood Marco.

Joseph blew out a long breath. "You know I don't want the life I have," he said, reiterating a truth he'd revealed long ago. "I didn't have a choice, Ashlyn. I was born into this world. I have no control over my choices. I do what my father tells me. I don't like it, but a fucked-up part of me still hates disappointing him."

I squeezed his hand. Joseph and I were more alike

than I'd ever realized. He felt pressure to make his father proud, just like I did. That desire had trapped him in a life, in a future, he didn't want.

Going to Harvard hadn't been my dream; it had been my father's. And while I enjoyed my studies, I'd chosen to go against my father's wishes and elected Art History as my major. He'd wanted me to major in Psychology and follow in his footsteps to a sensible career path. He'd made his disapproval clear: he would withhold his affection if I didn't make the choice that he thought was right. I'd considered changing my major.

But then, I'd met Joseph. He'd praised me for pursuing my passion over practicality. He'd allowed me to give myself permission to make the choice I wanted rather than cracking under my father's emotional blackmail.

Joseph felt the same way, the same sense of powerlessness. That was why he needed to dominate me. It was why he needed to feel in control when we were together, because he lacked it in every other aspect of his life.

"I want to try," I said softly. "The rope, I mean. I want to try it."

Joseph's eyes were bright with yearning. "Are you sure, angel?"

"How many times have I told you she's not made

of glass?" Marco said, growing impatient. He pulled me closer to his side, holding me tight. I leaned into him, welcoming the firm embrace. "Ashlyn was made for us, and you know it."

I no longer minded how they talked about me while I was with them. It was important for them to have these discussions, and I knew I had every right to speak up and voice my own opinion.

"Yes," I agreed. "I want to be with both of you. And I want to make you happy, Joseph. I want to give you what you need."

He traced the line of my jaw with his fingertips, touching me with awe. "Thank you, angel. I want to make you happy, too."

I gave him a soft smile. "I am happy."

It was true. I was happier than I'd ever been, despite the fact that I'd been ripped away from my life at Harvard. Joseph and Marco had taken me out of the life I didn't want and forced me to take a hard look at myself. I understood myself in ways I'd never realized I was missing. And while I still planned to return to a safer, simpler life when the danger passed, I was going to make some different choices. Choices that were made just for me, not to meet others' expectations of me.

Joseph returned my smile. "I'm glad, angel. We're

going to play now. If anything makes you uncomfortable or you want to stop, just say the word."

"I will. I trust you," I promised.

Joseph glanced at Marco, his smile widening to a wicked grin. "Do you want to carry our little captive upstairs, or should I?"

"I've got her," Marco said, his voice rumbling with a hint of a laugh.

He stood, taking me up with him as he settled my body over his shoulder. I giggled and relaxed against him, not even thinking about fighting as he carried me out of the media room. I could hear Joseph leading the way, but all I could see were Marco's boots moving across the floor in long, sure strides.

We made it up the stairs and into the bedroom within minutes. Joseph had headed in a different direction, but Marco sat down on the edge of the bed, arranging me so I sat in his lap. He tugged off my shirt and worked my pants down my legs. I was barefoot, so by the time he peeled them off my body, I was completely naked. Both men were still fully dressed, and I became very aware of the shifting power dynamic between us. They might be mine, but I was theirs to play with.

Joseph appeared in the doorway, holding a bulky gym bag.

"What's that?" I asked, puzzled.

He grinned. "My kit bag. This is where I keep all my toys."

He walked to the bed and set the bag down. Marco's hands closed around my elbows, and he drew my arms behind my back. At the same time, he hooked his boots around my ankles, forcing me to spread my legs. I was trapped, laid bare for Joseph's keen inspection. His pale eyes darkened, and he stared down at my body with hunger that bordered on obsession.

I wriggled in Marco's hold, and he nipped at my earlobe.

"Be still, little captive. Joseph wants to play with his pretty prisoner."

I watched as Joseph's cock stiffened at Marco's dark words, the hard ridge pressing against his jeans.

I knew I wasn't their prisoner. Not really. They might have kidnapped me and kept me on Marco's estate, but they were protecting me. Rather than frightening me, Marco was getting me hot. I liked knowing that I was powerless against them. They could do anything they wanted to me, and I wouldn't be able to stop them. What made my head spin with lust was the knowledge that they'd never hurt me, and everything they'd do to me would bring me pleasure.

Joseph unzipped his bag and reached in to retrieve a long strip of black cloth. I watched with rapt fascination as he wrapped it around his fist and lifted the soft material to my face, rubbing it against my cheek.

"Joseph's going to blindfold you," Marco murmured in my ear. "He wants you to focus on the feel of his ropes caressing your body for the first time. Don't worry about not being able to see, princess. I'll draw it for you later so you can see how pretty you look."

The warmth of his words fanned across my neck, and I shivered despite the heat. I stared up at Joseph, falling into his glowing aquamarine eyes. I'd never seen him look so... powerful. Self-assured. At peace.

I wanted to keep drinking him in, but he pressed the cloth over my eyes and knotted it at the back of my head. Darkness closed over me, and my skin pebbled as all my nerve endings crackled with awareness. For several long seconds, no one moved or spoke. I could still feel the heat of Marco's body against mine, could hear him breathing near my ear. I couldn't sense Joseph physically, but I could feel his power rolling over me. I felt small and deliciously vulnerable in his shadow.

A soft moan left my lips as desire overwhelmed

me. Marco chuckled and kissed my neck. I tilted my head to the side, welcoming more.

"I knew she'd be like this," he said to Joseph, his voice heavy with satisfaction. "You haven't even touched her yet, and I can feel her getting wet against my jeans."

I should have been mortified that my slick arousal was getting his pants damp, but he sounded so pleased with me that I couldn't be embarrassed.

I heard a shuffling sound, and I realized Joseph must have been retrieving something else from his bag. He touched something different to my cheek, a rougher material. The earthy scent of hemp surrounded me, and I sucked in a small gasp.

Rope.

Joseph really was going to tie me up. Before seeing Marco's drawings, I'd thought kinky couples might tie each other up. Something simple, like binding their wrists to the bedposts.

What I'd seen in Marco's sketches was far more intricate. The way the rope had bound me in his drawing had shaped and stretched my body, as though I were Joseph's work of art.

My pulse raced, and I could hear my heartbeat drumming in my ears. My mouth watered, and a small tremor raced across my skin.

Marco hummed against my neck, the sound

vibrating through my flesh. "I do love when you tremble, babygirl."

Joseph wasn't the only one who was hard. I could feel Marco's erection pressing into my ass. My pussy wept for him, aching for him to thrust into me and fill me like he had in the garden.

But I wanted Joseph, too. I wanted to feel his ropes around me.

The rough fibers shifted from my face. He trailed the rope over the top of my breast, and my nipples pebbled to hard peaks. I arched my back, straining toward the stimulation. When the rope brushed over my tight bud, I jerked and moaned at the hit of pleasure.

"You're perfect, angel," Joseph said, his voice deep with satisfaction. "You're going to love being in my ropes."

I wiggled against Marco, trying to rub my breasts against the rope again. He growled when I rubbed my ass against his erection.

"Go on, Joseph," he urged roughly. "Restrain our naughty little captive. If she keeps grinding on me like this, I'm going to come."

"Punish her if she's being naughty," Joseph said, his offhand tone implying it was a suggestion rather than a command. Marco seemed to be the one who issued orders, but Joseph was still thoroughly in control over me.

Marco kept my arms trapped behind my back with one hand. A harsh sting bloomed on my inner thigh when he slapped me with the other. I squealed and twisted against his hold, and he spanked me again.

"Be still," he growled in my ear.

When I didn't comply right away, his next slap landed directly on my spread pussy. Pleasure and pain lit up my system, my labia stinging even as the brief stimulation to my clit made me gasp in need.

I stopped moving against him, practically vibrating with the effort of holding myself still.

"Good girl." He nuzzled my cheek. "Don't tease Daddy."

A high whimper eased up my throat as lust rolled through me. Between Marco's dirty words and Joseph's toys, I was getting intoxicated. My mind began to float. All I could think about was *them*. Pleasing them. Being their good girl.

I couldn't see what Joseph was doing, but I wasn't nervous about that. Marco held me, and I was secure in his strong arms. I relaxed, staying in place for them. Marco kissed my hair, conveying his pleasure with my obedience.

I felt Joseph's fingertips skimming my sides just

before I felt the rope wrap around my chest, beneath my breasts. At first, it was little more than a soft caress. But as he began to wind the rope around me, it tightened, caging my body in an unfamiliar embrace. He wrapped it over my breasts, around the back of my neck, and down the center of my chest. He tugged, and I gasped as the rope tightened around my breasts. It didn't hurt, but I was very aware of the pressure on my sensitive flesh.

I felt him knot the rope at my back, finishing his work. I anticipated that he would continue to bind me, but he left my arms free, content to let Marco restrain me. He'd tied me up, but he hadn't restricted my movements in any way.

Even though he hadn't bound my arms, I still felt very much under his power. With each breath, I was aware of the rope that was wrapped around me. My breasts felt heavy, my nipples needy and throbbing for attention.

Marco's free hand stroked my inner thighs, teasing at the edge of my open pussy. That was enough to drive me wild, but when Joseph lightly trailed his fingers along the undersides of my breasts, pleasure flooded my system. I'd never been so sensitive, and the hit of bliss was strong enough to make me sag against Marco with a groan.

"I think she's ready for us," Joseph said.

Marco must have agreed, because he shifted me off his lap. I still couldn't see; all I could do was allow him to arrange my body the way he wanted. As he moved me, my breasts swayed in the ropes, making them feel strangely full and tender.

He placed me on my hands and knees, and I recognized the feel of the mattress sinking slightly beneath my weight. I felt their heat recede, heard the sound of clothing falling to the floor. Both my men were naked with me, but I couldn't see them. I wanted to admire them, and I shook my head, wishing I could shake the blindfold off.

I gasped when Marco palmed my breasts, his hands rubbing my tight nipples. Nothing had ever felt so decadent. My head dropped forward, suddenly too heavy to hold upright.

Marco continued playing with my breasts, and his other hand cupped my jaw, lifting my face.

"Tell Daddy how good it feels."

"So good, Daddy," I whimpered. My sex was wet and achy, but the stimulation of his hand on my bound breasts was enough to keep me on the edge of orgasm.

"Say *thank you* to Joseph," he commanded. "He's the one who put you in his pretty ropes."

"Thank you," I whispered, so drunk on pleasure that all I could do was obey.

Joseph's hand cracked across my ass, eliciting a sharp sting. He'd never spanked me before, but it didn't frighten me. It felt *good*. The burn from his palm sank through my flesh to heat my throbbing core.

"Thank you, *Sir*," he corrected me. "Marco might be your Daddy, but I'm your Master."

"What?" I asked faintly. Joseph might be domineering in the bedroom sometimes, but he was my sweet first love. The man who spoke to me now was more demanding. Darker.

Marco tweaked my nipple. "You heard him. Joseph's been holding back, but this is what he needs from you, babygirl. Now, thank him properly."

"Thank you, Sir." It should have felt weird, but I was too lost in bliss for anything to faze me.

Joseph stroked my ass, easing the sting of his slap.

I tensed when something hard and wet touched my asshole. I whined and tried to scoot away.

Marco's cock lightly slapped my cheek, an act of dominance and rebuke. I eased back into position without him having to tell me.

"Relax," he ordered. "Let Joseph stretch your tight little ass. He's been dying to fuck you there. This plug will help prepare you for that. We don't want to hurt you, princess. Now, take a breath and push back."

I obeyed, and the strange object penetrated my tight hole. It was slick with lubrication, but that didn't make it comfortable.

I whined and pressed my face against Marco, searching for comfort. He uttered a low curse when I nuzzled his hard cock.

"So sweet," he praised roughly, running his fingers though my hair while he continued to play with my breasts. "You're being so good for us, babygirl."

"It hurts, Daddy," I complained, struggling to adjust to the light burning sensation as the plug pressed deeper inside me.

"Touch her clit, Joseph. Make sure our girl enjoys this."

"Let me in, angel," Joseph coaxed me. He brushed his fingers over my clit, and ecstasy flashed through me. The plug slipped in a little farther, with minimal discomfort.

As he continued to stroke my clit and encourage me in his low, soothing tone, the burning sensation in my ass subsided. I began to relax, and he gently pumped the plug in and out of me. Dark pleasure rolled through me as Joseph touched me in this taboo way, preparing me for the day he'd put his cock in my ass.

The thought made my pussy clench, and the widest part of the plug slipped past my tight ring of muscles. It was seated deep inside me, filling me in a way I never would have imagined.

"So pretty," Joseph murmured, rubbing my clit harder. "Come for me, angel. Show me how much you like it when I stretch your tight asshole. Show me how you're going to come when I push my cock inside your ass for the first time."

The words were dirty, crass. Joseph had never spoken to me like this before. Marco had said Joseph had been holding back, and now I fully understood that he'd been leashing this darker side of himself. He'd been trying to protect me, shelter me.

But I didn't want him to hold back. I wanted all of him, even the dark parts. He needed this from me, and I needed him.

I came apart on a scream, my orgasm cresting in response to his firm touch on my clit and his crass talk.

As my pleasure rolled through me, I heard them murmuring how beautiful I was, how perfect and sweet. What we were doing should make me feel dirty, but I felt revered.

"I have to fuck her, Marco," Joseph growled as I began to come down.

"Do it. Our girl's going to learn how to suck Daddy's cock."

I heard a drawer opening, but Marco spoke

sharply. "Don't use a condom. She likes when you mark her with your cum." He touched two fingers beneath my chin. "You want Joseph to come deep inside your pussy, don't you, princess?"

"Yes, Daddy." I thrust my hips back toward Joseph. "Please, Sir."

My behavior was wanton, but it felt right. When I was surrounded by their heat, their power, I had no choice but to give myself to them in any way they desired.

The mattress dipped behind me, and I knew Joseph was getting ready to fuck my pussy. Marco's cock brushed across my lips, painting them with a drop of salty pre-cum.

"Kiss Daddy's cock, babygirl," he rasped.

He tugged the blindfold off my eyes, and I blinked to adjust to the sudden wash of light. When the world came into focus, I found Marco staring down at me, his eyes black with lust.

I remained locked in his gaze when I pressed a soft kiss against his cockhead, tasting more of his pre-cum. I lapped at it and opened my mouth to take him in. He hissed in a breath, and his fist tangled in my hair, pulling me away.

"No. Just kiss it."

For a moment, I didn't understand why he didn't want me to take him into my mouth. When I'd been with boys in the past, they'd wanted me to suck them off.

But Marco didn't want that. He wanted me to worship him first.

"That's it," he grunted as I began to slide my lips along his length, gliding my tongue against the underside. "Show Daddy how much you love his cock."

"Marco," Joseph snarled. His fingers curved into my hips, and his cock pressed against my wet entrance.

Marco tugged me back with his hold on my hair. "That was good, babygirl. But I think Joseph's waited long enough. I'm going to fuck your mouth while he stretches your tight little pussy. I want to feel you moaning around my dick. Open up."

My lips parted, and he slid inside my mouth. As his thick cock rubbed along my tongue, Joseph eased into my pussy. I whined as he entered me. With the plug stretching my ass, I felt almost unbearably full. It didn't hurt, but it was... intense.

"You feel that, angel?" Joseph asked, his voice tight with the effort of holding himself back. "It's going to feel even better when Marco is in your sweet pussy, and I'm inside your ass. We're going to fill you up and fuck you together. We're going to make you scream and come so hard you can't walk the next day.

Your body, your pleasure, they belong to us. *You* belong to us."

Marco pressed in farther, nearing the back of my throat. "Ours," he agreed, staring down at me. I suppressed my gag reflex, letting him in deeper. He groaned. "Fuck, babygirl. Fuck." His grip on my hair eased, and he started petting me. "Such a good girl. You make Daddy so happy."

I moaned around his cock as bliss suffused my system. Carnally, I was overwhelmed by sensation, but it was their words of pleasure and praise that sent me soaring.

He jerked inside my mouth, and he cursed again.

"Fuck her, Joseph," he ground out. "I can't take much more."

Joseph's hands firmed on my hips, and he thrust in hard, filling me to the hilt. He pressed against the base of the plug, driving it deeper into my ass. I cried out, and Marco growled as the sound tormented his dick. He kept one hand in my hair and reached beneath me with the other. I'd almost forgotten how sensitive my breasts had become with the rope still binding them, and I shrieked in shock when his fingers brushed over my aching nipples. Joseph fingered my clit at the same time, and my climax claimed me with ruthless force.

Mindlessly, I rocked back against Joseph while I

sucked Marco's cock. My inner muscles squeezed Joseph, and my scream vibrated down Marco's length. My ecstasy triggered theirs. Marco pressed deep into my throat, and I swallowed. His cum released into my mouth, just before Joseph's seed lashed into my pussy. I was marked, taken, owned.

The knowledge kept me riding high, and I floated on bliss as Joseph continued to drive into me, riding out the last of his orgasm.

Marco pulled out of my mouth, and I collapsed onto the mattress, gasping for breath. My sensitive breasts came into contact with the smooth sheets, and I whimpered. I couldn't manage to move my weight off them, so I simply trembled and rode out the pleasure that was coursing through me.

"Poor little princess," Marco cooed, smoothing my hair back from my cheek. "Let's get you out of Joseph's ropes."

He left me for a moment to get something from the kit bag. When he returned, he held a pair of blunt-tipped shears. He cut through the rope and uncoiled it from my body. Joseph pulled out of me and gently removed the plug. He went to the bathroom, and I heard running water before he returned a minute later.

Marco put the shears away, and Joseph rolled me onto my back. He stared down at me with awe, and he trailed his fingers along the little braided indentations the rope had left in my skin.

"So beautiful," he breathed.

"Yes," Marco agreed, joining us on the bed again.

They held me between their hard bodies, cuddling me close. I smiled and closed my eyes, sinking into bliss as they petted and praised me.

Chapter Ten
ASHLYN

Two Weeks Later

"I don't like this," Marco said, his face tight with worry. "We shouldn't take her off the estate."

In the last few weeks, Marco and Joseph had grown impossibly more possessive and protective. Now, Joseph's father insisted I come into the city to have dinner with their family. The three of us were about to leave our safe haven, and I couldn't deny that I was a little nervous. After all, our last foray into public had ended with me being threatened by their enemies.

"She'll be safe at my family's restaurant," Joseph

countered, but his eyes were clouded with worry as well. "No one would dare to touch her there."

"I know that," Marco replied. "It's what could happen on the way there and back that worries me."

"I can't put Dad off any longer," Joseph sighed. "He's been asking to meet Ashlyn for weeks. If we don't do this now, he might put his foot down and make me come back home. He's been letting me stay here with her at your family's estate. He's been letting me shirk my responsibilities. I don't want that to change."

"It's okay," I interjected. I didn't want Joseph to have to go back to his *responsibilities*. If being with me was giving him a valid excuse to stay away from his violent business, I didn't want to test his father. He might love Joseph, but that didn't mean he wouldn't force him into doing things that went against his true nature.

"We can go," I continued. "It's just dinner. I know you'll both keep me safe. I won't leave your sight."

It would simply be a matter of driving to the restaurant and then driving right back to the estate after dinner. There would be a brief window where I'd be on the street, moving inside from the car, but I had to trust that Joseph and Marco would protect me. They wouldn't let anyone come near me.

Marco's jaw ticked. "I still don't like it."

I wrapped my arms around him, letting him feel that I was safe with him. "Please, let's just go. I don't want Joseph to have to leave and stay with his family in the city. I need both of you here with me."

It was true. I needed both of them, and not just for protection. I'd become addicted to them, obsessed. They held me and cared for me and cherished me. I felt pampered and loved.

Loved.

I was falling in love with them. Both of them. I'd been ready to say it to Joseph weeks ago, but I'd held back once Marco joined our relationship. I knew it would hurt him if I declared my feelings for Joseph but not him.

I was swiftly coming to realize that I felt the same deep affection for both of them. It was unconventional, but that didn't make it any less true.

But now wasn't the time to say it. I'd tell them when we got back to the estate tonight. Everyone was tense, and this wasn't the moment to fall into their arms and confess my feelings.

I tucked my face against Marco's chest. "Please? Let's just go. I know you'll keep me safe."

He stroked my back. "Always, babygirl." He sighed. "I don't want Joseph to have to leave us, either. We can go to dinner."

"Thank you." I went up on my tiptoes and kissed him.

I felt Joseph's heat against my back. His hands settled around my waist, and he kissed my neck while Marco claimed my lips. The held me as though they couldn't get enough of me, and I definitely couldn't get enough of them.

Joseph's hands roved higher, moving toward my breasts.

I tore my mouth from Marco's. "We don't have time," I panted.

"My dad can wait," Joseph declared.

"No," I protested. "If we're going, let's go now. I don't want to test his patience."

"Dad's not like that," Joseph insisted. "He only wants to get to know you because he cares about me. He wants to meet my girlfriend."

"But if we don't go, he might make you come home and work for him," I countered quietly.

He stiffened. "Yes, that's a possibility."

"Then let's go. The sooner we leave, the sooner we can come back."

"Don't worry, Joseph," Marco rumbled. "I'll remember where we left off."

With that promise, they both stepped away from me. But each of them took one of my hands, unwilling to release me even for the walk to the garage.

They decided Marco would drive while Joseph sat with me in the backseat. Marco would have to park the car after dropping us off at the restaurant, and it made more sense for Joseph to go in with me. After all, I was supposed to be his girlfriend.

Girlfriend. The term didn't seem weighty enough to encompass my relationship with Joseph and Marco. And I didn't like that I was going to have to hide my feelings for Marco in front of Joseph's family.

Better get used to it, I told myself. If the three of us were going to be together, we'd have to put on a public front. Everyone knew I'd been with Joseph in Cambridge, so it was only logical that we posed as a couple.

It made my heart ache to think about Marco being left out. He would put on a tough face and pretend it didn't bother him, but I knew him better than that now. He needed affection, acceptance. Love. It would kill him to stand off to one side while Joseph got to hold me close in public.

I resolved to figure out that particularly difficult issue later. We just had to make it through this dinner, and then we could all discuss how to handle our relationship in public, once we got back to the privacy of Marco's estate. For now, I was Joseph's girlfriend, and that was all his family needed to see.

I rested my head on his shoulder during the ride into the city. Marco had finally told me the location of the estate—the North Shore of Long Island—a couple weeks ago. I'd had no idea that we were so close to the city, but I'd known Joseph and Marco could get there and back within a day.

By the time we arrived in the city, thick snowflakes were falling, dusting the sidewalks. I was grateful Joseph had provided me with more conservative, weather-appropriate clothes to wear. He might like when I wandered around the house in next to nothing, but he'd never let anyone other than Marco look at me when I wore so little. He was as possessive as ever, just not where Marco was concerned.

I hugged my pale pink pea coat tighter, shivering when Joseph opened the door and helped me out. I didn't have more than a few seconds to feel the cold; he hustled me into the restaurant in a matter of seconds, and Marco pulled away from the curb to find a parking spot.

Anxiety made my stomach knot, but I plastered on a pleasant smile. Meeting my boyfriend's parents would have been enough to make me nervous, but I knew Joseph's *family business*. His father was a career criminal, and anyone dining with us would be complicit to some degree or another. Joseph had promised me that his father was excited to meet me, but I was far from comfortable with the idea of meeting a mobster.

Well, a *real* mobster. Joseph and Marco didn't count.

Joseph led me through the restaurant after dropping off our coats with a young man at the host's stand. It was obvious that everyone who worked at the restaurant knew Joseph. They all had a polite smile and greeting for him.

When we reached a closed door at the back of the restaurant, Joseph opened it without hesitation and led me inside.

"Joseph!" a man's voice boomed, ringing with genuine joy.

I kept my body tucked halfway behind Joseph's, but I could see the older man get up from his seat at the head of the table. His face was blocky, his salt and pepper brows thick and heavy. He didn't look anything like Joseph, whose sensual features were practically sinful on a man. But their pale, aquamarine eyes were the same, and I knew this must be Joseph's father.

"Let me see her, let me see her." He waved Joseph to step aside as he approached us. His eyes caught on my face, and his features split in a wide, genuine smile. "You must be Ashlyn. *Bellissima*. No wonder my son's been hiding you away."

Even though I hadn't been able to greet him in return yet, he leaned in and clasped my shoulders, brushing a familiar kiss against my cheek before quickly pulling away. The energetic exchange occurred so fast, I could barely keep up.

"It's nice to meet you, Mr. Russo," I managed to find my ingrained manners. "Thank you so much for inviting me to dinner. Joseph's told me great things about your restaurant."

The door opened behind me, and I jolted slightly, on edge. Then, I felt Marco's fingers brush the small of my back as he came to stand beside me.

"Marco," Mr. Russo said with nearly the same enthusiasm he'd shown Joseph. "I'm glad you could come. Now it's a real family meal. Sit down, sit down."

He motioned us over to the dining table and resumed his seat at the head. The table was set for seven. To Mr. Russo's left, I noted a petite, middle-aged woman. Although fine lines were drawn around her eyes, it was obvious where Joseph's beautiful features and glossy black curls came from.

I gave her my best smile. "You must be Mrs. Russo. It's nice to meet you, too."

She inclined her head and returned my smile. "It's

nice to finally meet the girl who's stolen my son away." The words were a bit frosty, but she was outwardly polite.

My gaze flicked away from hers as my anxiety spiked. My eyes fell on the man seated on Mr. Russo's right. I instantly recognized him as Marco's father. They looked almost exactly the same, only separated by twenty years or so. Mr. De Luca even shared the same cold glint in his black eyes that Marco possessed. That hard exterior had frightened me at first, but I knew Marco better now. I knew he was gentle and kind.

I wasn't certain there was a gentle, kind soul hiding behind Mr. De Luca's hard exterior.

He gave me a small nod of acknowledgement. "Miss Meyers."

That was all he said in greeting. It was even frostier than what Mrs. Russo had offered me. In her case, I could understand the touch of animosity. Joseph had run away from his family and started a relationship with me in Cambridge. Even now, he was living at Marco's house with me instead of staying at his own home.

But Marco's father... He simply fixed me with a frozen stare, his cold eyes inspecting me.

Joseph pulled out a chair for me, seating me beside his mother. He settled down at the end of the table, opposite from his father, and Marco sat on Joseph's left. I wanted to be between them, but I knew that might seem odd. I did my best to smother my discomfiture.

"I'm Matt."

I blinked and focused on the final person seated at the table. A young man—he couldn't be older than eighteen—sat between Marco and his father. His wide smile seemed genuine, and I gratefully returned it. The boy didn't particularly resemble anyone at the table. He did seem to share Mrs. Russo's hazel eyes, but the similarities stopped there.

"Matt is my cousin," Joseph explained. "He's been helping my father while I've been with you."

I tried to keep the guilt out of my expression. This boy was being pulled into a life of violence because of me. If I hadn't been keeping Joseph away, Matt might be doing something different with his life. He might be enjoying his time like an eighteen-year-old boy should.

But I didn't want that violent life for Joseph, either. This little family gathering was only making me more determined than ever to get Joseph away from New York. I didn't care if his mother hated me for it.

That helped me brush off my anxiety over her obvious dislike.

The door opened again, and the young man from the host's stand stepped in, balancing drinks on a tray. He served Mr. Russo first, setting a glass of red wine in front of him. Mr. De Luca was next—a glass of whiskey. The rest of us received champagne.

"Are we celebrating something?" Joseph asked.

"Meeting Ashlyn, of course," his father replied, beaming at me. I was baffled. He really did seem excited to meet me. He might be a mobster, but he wasn't all that scary. Not like Marco's father.

He picked up his red wine in an obvious gesture that we were all meant to toast. I picked up my water glass rather than the champagne. I didn't want to drink alcohol. It might calm my nerves, but I needed to stay sharp. No matter how welcoming Mr. Russo might be, I couldn't let myself forget what he really was.

He frowned at me. "You don't like champagne?"

"Not really," I lied, taking the excuse he was giving me. "I'm good with water, but thank you."

"You have to at least toast," he told me. "Here. We'll trade, since you don't like champagne."

He passed his red wine to me. I thought about refusing, but Joseph squeezed my hand under the table.

"Thank you," I said, taking the glass from him and handing off my champagne flute.

He raised the flute, and the rest of us mirrored him. "To family," he toasted, meeting my eye with a significant glance. It was bizarre, feeling so welcomed by a man I knew was dangerous.

To be polite, I took a sip of the red wine. I supposed I'd have to drink a little more over the course of the meal, since Joseph had grabbed my hand to signal for me to take it in the first place. While his father was jovial, there was clearly some underlying tension. Obviously, no one said *no* to Mr. Russo.

"So, Ashlyn," he addressed me. "Joseph tells me you're a student at Harvard. That's very impressive."

I blushed, heat creeping up my neck. "Thank you."

"What are you studying?"

I flushed hotter, anticipating that Mr. Russo would react similarly to my own father regarding my choice of major. After all, it wasn't very practical.

"Art History," I told him.

His brows rose with interest rather than condemnation. "And what do you want to do with that?"

His scrutiny was making me uncomfortable, and I was very aware of everyone's eyes on me. My sweater was suddenly far too hot, and my palm grew clammy against Joseph's.

"I thought I might work in a museum or a gallery for a while," I replied.

My stomach twisted violently, and I stifled a gasp. I'd never had a nervous reaction this intense before. Then again, I'd never been surrounded by mobsters before. Maybe I was on the verge of a panic attack.

Whatever it was, I needed to excuse myself before I freaked out in front of everyone.

"You okay, angel?"

"Yeah," I said shakily. "I um, I just need the restroom. Excuse me."

My body burned with embarrassment. Sweat beaded on my brow, and I pushed up out of my chair.

I didn't make it two steps before pain knifed through my gut, intense enough to knock the air from my lungs and make my knees weak. Joseph was with me in an instant, catching me before I collapsed.

"Sorry," I said faintly. "I don't know—"

I doubled over on a harsh cry as my stomach twisted again. Acid coated my tongue, and a foamy substance dripped from my lips.

I was vaguely aware of Marco shouting for an ambulance, Joseph saying my name over and over again. My body convulsed, pain wracking my senses as everything faded to black.

Chapter Eleven
JOSEPH

I paced back and forth across the hospital waiting room, my gut twisting with fear I'd never known before.

Poison. Ashlyn had taken the poison meant for my father.

She could die.

I didn't understand how Marco could bear sitting still in the tiny waiting room chair. His face was ashen, his eyes staring at something far away that I couldn't see.

Inexplicable rage surged. How could he sit there when Ashlyn's life hung in the balance? How could he hunch his shoulders like he'd already given up on her?

"She's going to be fine," I growled at him, even though I didn't fully believe it. I had to say it out loud, because Marco looked like he was already at her fucking funeral.

He scrubbed a hand over his face. "My fault," he muttered, and I was certain he hadn't meant to say the words aloud.

In my anger, I caught on to the admission. We weren't sure who had slipped the poison into my father's wine, but if Marco knew who was responsible, he'd better spill. If he was holding back on us for some reason, I'd kick his teeth in. Fury coursed through me, desperate for an outlet. Taking it out on the motherfucker who was responsible for this would be a good start.

"What do you mean?" I barked. "Do you know who did this?"

He finally looked at me, his black eyes drawn with anguish. "I did."

I wasn't sure what he was playing at or who he was trying to protect, but that simply couldn't be true. "What do you know about this? Tell me right fucking now, Marco."

His gaze shifted. His eyes met mine, but he was focused on something I couldn't see again.

"I did this," he rasped. "I took her. I brought her into our world."

"Fuck off," I seethed. I didn't need any melodramatic bullshit right now. "You know we didn't have a choice. She was in danger."

"She wasn't. But I took her anyway."

I froze. "What the fuck are you talking about?"

He blinked and stared at me again, but his eyes were hollow. "You were so unhappy without her. So, I gave her back to you."

"I don't know what you're trying to say, but you'd better start making sense. Snap the fuck out of it. You know our enemies were watching her. They were going to hurt her to get to me."

"They weren't," he said on a strained whisper. "I didn't know that for sure. I knew it was a possibility they'd been watching you in Cambridge, but there wasn't a threat against her after you left. Not really."

My mind churned, struggling to absorb what he was saying. Marco wouldn't betray me like that. He wouldn't pull Ashlyn into our world without a good reason. Not when he knew I'd left her behind to protect her.

"But Ricky threatened her at the restaurant when we took her off the estate. He said they had pictures of us together. They'd been watching the estate since we took her."

"They might have known about your relationship in Cambridge, but they had no reason to think you still cared for her after you left her behind. She probably wasn't on their radar until I brought her to you."

"You can't know that for sure," I said, still unable to process the depth of his betrayal.

He surged to his feet, getting in my face. "This is my fault, Joseph. Why aren't you listening to me? It's my fucking fault. And now she might die. She—"

Whatever he was going to say next was cut off when my fist connected with his jaw. I didn't hold back, and he reeled at the force of the blow. He staggered and shook his head hard to clear it.

He didn't tense with aggression. He didn't take a defensive stance.

He simply stared at me, as though he wanted me to hit him again, to punish him for his unforgivable sin.

"Hey!" A security guard appeared in the waiting room. "Break it up. You're both going to have to leave."

Marco rubbed his jaw and turned away from me. "I'm going," he told the man. "Joseph can stay."

I watched as he stalked off down the long hallway. My stomach dropped, and my chest hollowed out.

Marco had betrayed me. He'd put the woman I loved in danger, for his own selfish reasons.

No, he'd done it for me.

And that only made his choice that much more

inexcusable. He'd made me complicit in this. It was equally my fault that Ashlyn was fighting for her life right now. Because I'd chosen to keep her with me instead of sending her to the police for protection. Marco's reasoning that we were protecting her was just a flimsy excuse for me to keep her. I'd wanted her to be mine, so I'd taken her.

"Mr. Russo?" A nurse in green scrubs called my name.

She's not dead, I told myself in the long second it took for the man to speak. *She's not dead.*

"Miss Meyers is stable. She's going to be okay. You can come see her if you want."

My knees almost went out from under me as relief slammed through my body. My legs shook as I followed the nurse to her hospital room, but somehow, I managed to walk without stumbling.

When I got to her room, I rushed to her side, taking her small hand in mine. It was warm, reassuring me that she was alive. But the pretty pink flush was absent from her cheeks, and her full lips were chapped and pale.

She stirred when I stroked my thumb over her palm.

"Joseph?" she mumbled. She didn't open her eyes, and I wasn't sure if she was fully awake. She certainly wasn't completely aware of her surroundings. I'd always known she was fragile, but it pained me to see her so frail.

"I'm right here, angel," I promised. "I'm not going anywhere."

"Where's Marco?" she slurred.

Rage made my muscles ripple and flex, but I was careful not to squeeze her delicate hand.

"Go to sleep, angel," I said instead of answering her. "You need to rest."

A little furrow persisted between her brows, but a few seconds later, it eased. Her breathing turned deep and even.

My eyes burned.

Our fault.

My fault.

I never should have kept her for myself. For *us*.

It was too late to send her back to the safety of her life at Harvard. That was shattered now that my father's enemies were aware that she was with me. They knew she was important to me because I'd brought her to New York.

Because *Marco* had brought her to New York.

I'd been angry with him in the past, but I'd never felt this toxic rage. It held a sharp edge of hatred that shredded my insides.

I might have no choice but to take Ashlyn back to the safety of his family's estate, but what Marco and I had shared was broken. He wasn't my brother anymore, and Ashlyn would never belong to him. She was mine, and mine alone.

~

It had been three days since I'd brought Ashlyn back to the estate, but she was still weak, and she tired easily. Really, she should still be in the hospital, but I didn't want to risk her. She was safest on Marco's estate, behind the impenetrable gates.

We'd arranged for an on-call doctor come check on her twice a day. Other than that, I took care of her.

And Marco kept his fucking distance, as he should.

She'd asked for him several times, but I'd told her he was busy in the city, helping my father track down the fuckers who had tried to poison him. Of course, we knew who was ultimately responsible, but we couldn't go after Gabriel Costa until someone turned on him. Whoever had tried to poison Dad had to say they were working under Costa's orders. Otherwise, we'd be the ones instigating the war, and the family might not survive that. It was essential that my father came out on top, with the family intact and as powerful as ever.

I was grateful that the task of finding the traitor kept Marco away, but part of me wanted to help. Twice, Marco had returned with blood on his hands, his knuckles split. He got to be out there, hurting the people who had hurt Ashlyn. And while I didn't like my violent lifestyle, I wouldn't mind beating the shit out of whoever was responsible for almost taking her from me.

As it was, Marco only showed his face if he was bringing Ashlyn's meals to her in the bedroom. He wisely left them on the nightstand and let me feed her. If he tried to pull any Daddy shit with her in front of me, I'd punch him again. He didn't get to be her Daddy. He didn't get to take on that responsibility. He'd lost the privilege.

Ashlyn seemed upset when he'd leave, but mostly, she slept.

Today, she was brighter, more alert. She'd been awake for nearly three hours this afternoon, and she was sitting in bed, propped up against the pillows. I'd brought a TV in from one of the guest bedrooms so we could watch *Sons of Anarchy* together. I sat in bed beside her, and she rested her head on my shoulder.

I couldn't stop touching her, couldn't stop feeling her warmth and inhaling her light, floral scent. I'd almost lost her, and I had to reassure myself that she was alive and safe in my arms.

Marco knocked on his bedroom door, waiting for me to invite him to enter. When I did, he stepped into the room, carrying two steaming plates of pasta. He'd been cooking blander dishes for Ashlyn, making sure she could keep the food down while still getting enough calories.

He set the plates on the nightstand, not looking at either of us.

"Marco," Ashlyn said, her voice soft and pleading. "Come sit with us."

He tensed, but he jerked his head in silent refusal and turned away. She reached out and caught his wrist.

"Wait. Don't go. I want to talk to you."

"I'm sorry," he rasped and pulled his hand free from her weak grip.

"Come back." I was sure she meant to sound firm, but she was still too weak to put any real force behind the demand.

He kept walking, his movements stiff but determined.

"Daddy, please. I need you."

He froze, and I tensed.

"It's okay, angel." I tried to sound soothing. "Marco can't stay." I made that sharper, letting Marco know he wasn't welcome.

"No!" she insisted. "I need you. Both of you. Please stay, Marco."

My arm firmed around her. "He doesn't deserve to be here."

Marco turned to face her. His eyes were tight with anguish, but his distress did little to melt my icy rage.

"He's right," Marco said. "I don't deserve you. I'm sorry."

"Of course you do," she said. "We're supposed to be together. All of us."

"You don't know what he did," I ground out.

"Whatever it is, I don't care," she declared. She reached for Marco, her fingers straining toward him, beseeching. "I love you, Marco. Please, don't go."

All the air left my chest, but before ugly jealousy could rise, she turned her sapphire eyes on me.

"And I love you, Joseph. I love both of you. I need both of you." She looked back at Marco. "Please, Daddy. Don't go."

He groaned and closed the distance between them, unable to resist her allure when she admitted her need for him. He knelt by the bed and took her hand in both of his, holding her carefully.

"I can't be with you, babygirl," he forced out. "You're supposed to be with Joseph. I'm not good for you."

"I've told you before, but I guess you forgot," she said, her voice gaining a little strength. "You deserve to be loved, Marco. And I love you, just the way you are. No matter what."

His eyes were dark with pain and longing. "But I kidnapped you. I brought you here, and now you're in danger."

"I was in danger before you took me. That's why you brought me here, isn't it? And when the danger has passed, we can go back to Cambridge. All of us."

My heart squeezed. Ashlyn had created a pretty little fantasy in her mind. It was past time I gave her the truth about her future.

"We might never be able to go back, angel," I said quietly. "You weren't under threat at Harvard. Not after I left. But Marco took you anyway. And I chose to keep you. Now, you might not ever be able to go back. And it's our fault."

Our fault. Not just Marco's. Because I'd done this to her, too. From the moment I'd first met her, I'd wanted her. I'd tried to stay away, but eventually, I broke down. Selfishly, I started a relationship with her, even though I knew it was dangerous for her to associate with me. Just because I'd tried to leave her behind in Cambridge, that didn't absolve me.

"I never should have come near you," I admitted, my strain matching Marco's. We were both at fault, and now Ashlyn's life would never be the same. "You might never get to go back. You might never be able to have the life you wanted."

"That wasn't the life I wanted," she said firmly. "You helped me see that. I made choices to meet other people's expectations of me. That's not how I want to live my life. I want to make my own choices. I want to be with the two of you. Don't you want to be with me?" She softened on the last, suddenly uncertain.

"Of course we want to be with you, princess," Marco said. "But we shouldn't—"

"Don't tell me what I should and shouldn't do," she said with sudden ferocity. "I get to make my own choices from now on, and I choose you and Joseph. We can figure the rest out later. I love you. Both of you."

I love you. I'd waited so long to hear those words fall from her perfect lips.

"I've always loved you, Ashlyn," I admitted. I'd known she was mine from the moment I laid eyes on her. My complicated life had kept me at a distance from her, but I couldn't hold back any longer.

"I love you too, babygirl," Marco said with the weight of an oath.

She smiled and sank back into the pillows. "Good. Now, get in bed and cuddle with us. We can put on

Parks and Recreation, if you want," she offered, knowing Marco preferred comedies.

He gave her a lopsided grin. "You have to eat your dinner first, princess. Then, we can cuddle all you want."

My best friend was back; the self-destructive, miserable man he'd become over the last few days was gone. I was happy to see that man go.

"Marco," I said his name solemnly, calling his attention to me. "I'm sorry for punching you. I owe you one."

Now that we'd earned Ashlyn's forgiveness and love, I couldn't hate Marco. I couldn't regret my choices or his actions, because they'd brought Ashlyn into our lives.

"No one's punching anyone," she interjected firmly.

Marco chuckled. "Okay, princess. Whatever you say."

Ashlyn might do as we told her, but we'd do anything for her. She was ours, but we belonged to her.

Chapter Twelve
ASHLYN

I loved my men, and they loved me. They'd made that clear over the last week, both of them doting on me as I recovered my full strength. Neither of them had left my side for more than a few minutes since we'd confessed our feelings for one another. Both Marco and Joseph had ignored their fathers' calls. I knew my men were expected to help look for the people responsible for poisoning me, but they cared more about seeing to my needs than serving their fathers.

Good. It was past time we all started living for ourselves instead of bowing to pressure from our parents. After all, I hadn't been the target of the poisoning. If someone was out to get Joseph's father, that was his business.

I let out a happy little hum as I sank into the warm bath. Ever since we'd all admitted our love for one another, Marco had been more attentive than ever. He took his responsibilities for my wellbeing very seriously. Between Joseph's constant affection and Marco's daily pampering, I felt like the luckiest woman in the world.

"It's not too hot is it, babygirl?" Marco asked as the water level rose higher, fluffy bubbles covering my abdomen.

"It's perfect."

I smiled up at him where he knelt beside the tub. At first, I'd thought it was odd that he didn't want to get in the massive bath with me. But I'd quickly realized that he wanted to take care of me. This was more than sensual play for him. It was an essential part of who he was. He needed this from me: my trust, my love.

He returned my smile and reached for the showerhead that was attached to the faucet. He'd never done that before. Usually, he massaged my shoulders and washed my hair while I languished in the warm water. This time, he'd piled my hair on top of my head in a bun, keeping it from getting wet.

When the bath was only half-full, he turned the knob so the water sprayed from the showerhead. He directed the spray away from my body while he squirted body wash onto a pink loofa.

He brushed the soapy loofa over my shoulders, applying light pressure at my nape as he rubbed in soothing little circles. My eyes slid closed, and I reveled in the feel of Marco caressing my body.

He continued to gently scrub my skin, making his way down my chest to tease around my breasts. Despite the warmth of the bath, my nipples pebbled, aching for attention. The loofa brushed over the tight peaks, and I arched forward with a gasp.

His low chuckle rumbled through me, the pleasure in the sound making warmth flood my chest.

Then, the heated spray from the showerhead hit my breasts, and my head tipped back on a moan.

Marco kept the water directed at my chest, stimulating my nipples while he worked his way lower with the loofa. It dipped below the waterline, and he rubbed it over my swollen pussy. I let my thighs fall open, welcoming him to wash me in this erotic way.

My eyes flew open when he pushed the loofa back farther, stimulating my sensitive asshole. At the same time, he brought the showerhead down so the spray landed directly on my clit.

My fingers scrabbled at the edges of the tub, searching for something to hold onto as I cried out at the shock of pleasure.

Marco laughed again, the sound rich with satisfaction. "Let's get you nice and clean for Joseph, princess."

My lashes fluttered as ecstasy pulsed through me, and I struggled to focus on him. "What?" I asked faintly.

"Joseph and I discussed it, and we decided you're ready. For both of us."

The thought of both of them penetrating me at the same time sent a fresh wave of lust rolling through my body, and I moaned. They hadn't touched me sexually while I'd been recovering, but prior to that, they'd worked to prepare my body to take Joseph's cock in my ass.

I squirmed in the water, and Marco took the showerhead away from my clit.

"No!" I gasped, grabbing for it. I'd been close to orgasm, and he'd denied me.

"Greedy girl," he laughed. "We have to wait for Joseph."

He rubbed the loofa over my asshole again, giving me just enough stimulation to make me crave more.

"You're being mean." I pouted.

He kissed my forehead. "You're going to come so hard for Daddy and Joseph. No orgasms before we're both inside you."

Mercifully, he took the loofa away and rinsed the soap off my torso with the warm spray. I tried to relax against the tub, but he'd gotten me worked up, and now my muscles were tight with sensual need.

"Come on, babygirl. Joseph's waiting for us."

He helped me out of the tub and dried me off with a fluffy white towel. The soft material rubbed over my peaked nipples and swollen pussy, but Marco didn't linger to give me more pleasure; he gave me just enough to keep me hot and needy.

When I was dry, he didn't give me anything to wear. He removed the pins from my hair, releasing the bun so my dark locks fell loose around my shoulders. He took my hand in his and opened the bathroom door, leading me into the bedroom.

Joseph sat up from where he'd been lounging against the headboard. He wore only a pair of low-slung gray sweatpants, leaving his powerful torso on display. As he moved toward me, his muscles rippled and flexed. My mouth watered, and my sex grew damp as my need grew more intense. Marco had just dried me off, but my thighs were slick with arousal already.

He stopped when he reached me, curling two fingers beneath my chin to lift my face to his.

"Did Marco get you ready for me, angel?"

I blushed, but I didn't look away. "Yes, Sir." It already felt natural to address him with respect when we were playing kinky games.

His eyes sparked with pleasure, and he leaned in to take my lips in a slow, reverent kiss.

Marco's heat receded slightly, and I heard his clothes falling to the floor. When Joseph released me from his kiss, I turned so I could admire Marco. He was even more solidly built than Joseph. The strength that had once intimidated me now made my heart flutter and my core heat. I licked my lips as I took my time to admire his ripped abs, his corded thighs, his heavy, hard cock.

Joseph took my hand and pressed it against his own erection, and I realized he'd stripped as well. We were all naked together, bare for each other.

I didn't think I'd ever get enough of this, enough of *them*.

And they were studying me with the same mix of hunger and wonder.

"Do you feel how much we want you, angel?" Joseph asked roughly as I closed my hand around his shaft and stroked him.

Marco took my other hand and wrapped it around his cock, so I was holding both of them. A sense of feminine power rolled over me, intoxicating me.

They might be in control, but they were *mine*. This arousal was for me, and me alone.

Marco's growl mingled with Joseph's low groan when I pressed my thumbs against the undersides of their dicks, teasing just beneath their cockheads.

The both caught my wrists at the same time, pulling my hands away. Marco landed a swift swat against my ass. Stinging heat bloomed on my skin before sinking deeper into my flesh.

"Naughty," he reprimanded. He glanced up at Joseph. "Our girl thinks she can tease us. I think you should punish her this time."

"I'd be happy to. I haven't had a reason to spank her in a while. She's been so good for us." His tone lilted with wicked pleasure. Marco might discipline me when I'd been naughty, but Joseph got a different, darker pleasure out of making my bottom red.

Marco kept his hold on my wrist and led me over to the bed. He left me standing at the edge while he settled down on his back, leaning against the pillows.

"Make her ride my cock, Joseph. I want to feel her pussy squeezing me while you spank her."

Joseph's hands closed around my waist, guiding me up onto the bed. He settled me on my knees so I straddled Marco's hips.

Marco fisted his cock, directing it to my slick opening. Joseph pushed me down slowly, lowering me onto Marco. Pleasure sizzled through me as he slowly stretched me. I tried to move faster, but Joseph controlled the achingly slow pace, allowing me to feel each inch of Marco penetrating me.

When he was finally in to the hilt, Marco's hand closed around my nape, pulling me toward him for a fierce kiss. My hands pressed into the pillow on either side of his head as I sought to balance my body weight.

I gasped into his mouth when Joseph's hand cracked across my ass cheeks, one and then the other. My pussy fluttered around Marco, and he snarled against me. The sound of his lust vibrated into my mouth before making its way deeper into my body, reaching my core.

Marco tore his lips from mine. "Don't do that again," he warned Joseph. "She likes it too much, and I won't be able to hold back. I want to fuck her together."

"Are you sorry for teasing us?" Joseph asked me in his deepest, darkest tone.

"Yes, Sir," I whispered, completely overwhelmed by them. My body quivered in anticipation of being fucked by both of them. I craved and feared it. I knew they wouldn't hurt me, but wasn't certain I could handle the intensity of being filled simultaneously.

Joseph didn't give me time to worry. He reached over onto the nightstand and pumped lube into his hand before sliding it over his cock. Then, he positioned himself behind me on the bed. Marco gripped my stinging ass cheeks in both hands, spreading me wide and offering me to Joseph.

My arms shook, barely able to balance my body over Marco's. I stared down at him, captured in his deep, dark stare.

"Are you ready, babygirl?" he murmured, achingly gentle despite his unforgiving grip on my bottom.

"Yes, Daddy." I was nervous, but I was ready. I wanted both my men to claim me.

Marco throbbed inside me, and Joseph pressed against my asshole. I tensed on instinct, and Marco's fingers firmed on my bottom.

"Open up, princess. Let Joseph in."

I took a breath and tried to relax. My entire body trembled with sensual tension, but I pushed back toward Joseph, inviting him in. The pressure against my tight hole increased, his thick cockhead breeching my ring of muscles. He was much bigger than the last plug I'd taken, and a burning sensation accompanied the slow penetration.

I whined and tried to wiggle away, but Marco kept me locked in place.

"You're okay, babygirl. We've got you."

Joseph reached around me and strummed my clit, the hit of pleasure helping me relax. His cockhead slipped past my tight ring, and some of the unbearable pressure eased. My head dropped forward onto Marco's chest, and I panted against him, little whimpers leaving me with each exhale.

He finally released my bottom so he could stroke my back.

"You're doing so well," he praised. "Such a good girl."

Joseph continued to push forward, stretching me slowly. "That's it, angel," he coaxed. "You can take us."

I squirmed between them, completely overwhelmed as they filled me. There was nowhere for me to go, no escape from their unyielding bodies. All I could do was soften and submit. As Marco continued to stroke me and Joseph teased my clit, I took deep breaths and tried to accommodate them.

I felt Joseph enter me fully, and both men paused, remaining completely still within me. We were all breathing hard; my men panting with the effort of holding back, and I sucked in deep breaths to try to keep myself centered. I felt like I could shatter into a million pieces if the tension in my body broke. Their firm hands were the only things holding me together, tethering me to sanity.

Then Joseph moved, and my eyes rolled back in my head as pleasure washed over me. He slowly pulled out, his thick cock dragging almost all the way free before he slid back in. Without realizing, I bit into Marco's shoulder, muffling my desperate whine. He hissed in a breath, but his hand closed around the back of my head, inviting me to cling onto him with my teeth.

Joseph gripped my waist, urging me to move against Marco. With the first shift of my hips, Marco's cockhead hit my g-spot, and my muscles convulsed at the surge of bliss. Both men cursed, and Joseph's movements became faster, rougher. Marco rocked his hips up into me, driving deeper.

I cried out against Marco's neck, tasting the salt of his skin on my lips. We were all covered in a thin sheen of sweat, our bodies sliding together as our rhythm became wilder, more primal. We fucked with wild abandon, each of us clawing our way toward the peak. My gasps and moans mingled with their grunts and growls, and they started to take me more harshly. My body stretched and opened to accommodate them. There was no more discomfort; just an overwhelming sense of fullness and a burning *need*.

I shattered first, throwing my head back on a long wail as my pussy and ass contracted around them. Ecstasy ripped through me with ruthless force, lighting up my entire body with transcendent bliss. The world went white as lighting burst across my vision. When it began to clear, I looked down into Marco's eyes. They were black with lust, strained with his own need. I wanted him to come undone. I wanted his cum inside me. I wanted both of them to mark me.

Riding out the aftershocks of my pleasure, I clenched my muscles around them. Joseph cursed, and I felt his hot seed emptying deep inside me. His fingers curled into my hips as he held me fast, pumping into me for a few more brutal strokes.

Marco finally let go, letting out a wordless roar as he rocked his hips toward me, driving deep as he filled me with his cum.

"What the fuck?"

I shrieked at the sound of the stranger's voice, shock ripping through my pleasure.

"Matt," Marco rasped, looking past me toward the threshold to the bedroom. "This isn't—"

"You're a fucking fag," the boy spat out. "Your father sent me here to find out why you haven't been taking his calls. I heard screaming, and I thought something was wrong. But you... Both of you... You're fucking fags," he hurled the insult again.

Joseph cursed, and but he moved with slow care

as he pulled out of me. I could hear footsteps pounding down the staircase. Matt was running away.

"Fuck, fuck," Joseph repeated, frantic. He lifted me off Marco, still handling me carefully so he didn't hurt me. "Go after him, Marco. We have to explain. We can't let him tell anyone."

"I know," Marco said grimly, getting to his feet and yanking on his jeans.

I heard tires squealing against asphalt outside. Marco looked out the window, then shook his head.

"He'll be out the gates before I can get to him." He turned back to look at me, his face paler than I'd ever seen it. "Clean up and get dressed. We have to get into the city and do damage control."

"I thought it wasn't safe to leave the estate," I said, but I started to climb out of bed.

He shook his head sharply. "We can't stay here. They'll come right for us. We have to head them off and try to explain."

"But why?" I asked, not understanding why the situation was so dire. Of course, it was odd for the three of us to be together. But Marco made it sound as though we were in danger.

"Homosexuality isn't accepted in our world," Joseph told me, just as grim as Marco. "If my father's enemies catch wind of this, it'll be all the excuse they need to come after my family."

"But you're not gay," I said. What we shared didn't really have a definition that I was familiar with, but we were all together. The three of us.

"They won't see it that way," Marco said. "Come on. We have to go. We have to get to Matt before he turns on us."

Chapter Thirteen
ASHLYN

"Why are we splitting up?" I asked Joseph as we pulled through the open gates that guarded Marco's estate.

Marco zoomed past the Porsche on his motorcycle, already speeding toward the city.

Joseph hit the gas, following him. For now.

I didn't like that we weren't all in the car together. I didn't like that we were about to go in different directions.

"You and I need to get to my father at the restaurant," Joseph explained. "Matt might've already called him to tell him what he saw, but we need to try to get to him first. We have to explain."

"And what are we going to say?" I asked, concerned. "Will your father accept that the three of us are together?"

His knuckles turned white on the steering wheel. "Probably not. But it might make enough of a difference that he'll protect us from the rest of the family." He glanced over at me. "I hate that I'm bringing you into this, but I can't leave you alone on the estate without one of us to protect you. Just stay close to me."

"But what about Marco? Where is he going?"

"He's going to try to find Matt, if he hasn't gone to the restaurant. If we're lucky, Matt will go straight to my father."

"And if we aren't lucky?"

His jaw ticked. "Matt might decide to go to Gabriel Costa, my father's rival. He might forsake our blood family for what I've done."

"But I don't understand why it's so terrible."

He reached over and squeezed my hand. "It's not. There's nothing wrong with what we share. But other people in my world won't see it that way." He returned his grip to the steering wheel and pressed down on the gas. "Hold on, angel. We're about to break a few laws."

∼

Joseph pulled up to the curb in front of his family's restaurant. I was sure the parking ticket he would get would be far less expensive than all the traffic violations he'd committed getting us here. It was a miracle we hadn't been pulled over, but I was fairly certain he'd be getting a ticket for running at least one red light.

My heart pounded in my chest from the frightening ride. Joseph had seemed in control the whole time, but the speed had still been unnerving.

He opened my car door and helped me out, shielding my body with his as we crossed the sidewalk to the restaurant entrance.

"Shit," he cursed under his breath.

The place was deserted, the lights off. The sign on the glass door was flipped to *closed*.

It was six in the evening. The restaurant should be open and packed with patrons. My stomach turned with anxiety, and I noted that Joseph's fingers shook slightly as he found the right key attached to the car keys. He slid it into the lock on the front door, and we stepped into the darkened space.

Light peeked around the outline of the door to the private room at the back of the restaurant, where I'd shared dinner with Joseph's family on the night I was poisoned. Muffled voices floated through the closed door, and Joseph shifted his body in front of mine.

"Stay behind me," he ordered, his voice barely above a whisper.

I fell into step behind him as we crossed the eerily empty restaurant. I expected the voices to become clearer as we neared the door, but it seemed it had been built to block sound. The people on the other side must be shouting for us to be able to hear them at all.

My unease intensified.

They know. Matt must have told Joseph's father already, and he must be furious.

I took a deep breath. *It'll be fine,* I told myself. *We'll explain, and it'll be fine.*

I remembered how happy Mr. Russo had been to meet me, the genuine joy in his eyes when he'd greeted Joseph. He loved his son. He wouldn't allow anyone to hurt Joseph.

Something hard jammed into my ribs, and I cried out at the shock of pain. The sound was immediately smothered when a hand clamped over my mouth.

Fear slammed through my system. I didn't have to see it to identify the hard object pressed against the side of my chest: a gun.

Joseph turned, but it was too late. My captor jerked me back, out of his reach.

Joseph froze, his face going pale as his eyes focused on the gun at my side.

"Let her go, Ricky," he demanded. "She has nothing to do with this."

"That's not what I heard." I recognized the voice: the man who had threatened me in the bathroom when Joseph and Marco had taken me out to dinner. "I heard she was part of your little fuck fest." I heard him inhale near my hair, breathing in my scent. "She smells so sweet to be such a dirty bitch."

Joseph snarled and took a step forward. I winced when Ricky dug the gun deeper into my side.

Joseph froze again, his body vibrating with suppressed violence.

"Go on in," Ricky told him. "Your old man is waiting for you."

"You don't work for my father," Joseph said. "You work for Costa. Why are you here?"

The pressure of the gun eased slightly just before it slammed back into my ribs. My pained cry caught against his hand, and Joseph's face twisted with rage.

"Go in," Ricky repeated, his tone silky with vindictive malice. "We'll be right behind you."

Joseph reached behind him for the doorknob, but he didn't turn away from me. He kept his eyes trained on the gun at my side.

He was so busy watching me that he didn't see the man waiting on the other side of the door. He didn't see the flash of steel just before the knife slammed into his lower back. His eyes flew wide, his mouth falling open. For a second, he didn't make a sound.

Then, the man wrenched the knife free, and Joseph fell to his knees with a harsh shout.

I screamed and twisted against Ricky's hold, struggling to get to the man I loved. I managed to get my mouth free from beneath his hand, and I sank my teeth into his fingers. He released me with a curse, but I didn't get a step away from him before the gun slammed into the side of my head.

Pain cracked through my skull, and I heard Joseph say my name.

The world flickered around me, and I blinked hard, willing everything to stop spinning.

I realized I was on the floor, my cheek pressed against cool tiles. Something warm and wet trickled through my hair, but I couldn't think about that.

All I could focus on was Joseph's pale face, his gorgeous features drawn tight with pain and panic. He struggled to his feet, but Ricky pushed him back down with a hard shove to his shoulder and trained his gun on the back of Joseph's head.

Gritting my teeth against the pounding pain in my skull, I tried to stand, to go to Joseph.

I didn't make it to my knees before a man's hand tangled in my hair, jerking me up to my feet.

"Let the girl go, Gabriel," Mr. Russo demanded.

I struggled to get my bearings. Joseph's father sat in his chair at the head of the table, but a man stood behind him, with a gun pressed against the side of his skull.

"I don't think so," the man holding me—Gabriel—said. "I was going to finally kill you, Dominic. When everyone finds out your son's a fag, no one would bat an eye at eradicating your family. You're obviously too weak to take Lombardi's place. But I don't think I'll have to kill you, after all. Are you going to cry, Dominic?"

Mr. Russo's eyes were shining as he stared at Joseph. No matter his feelings about Joseph allegedly being gay, Mr. Russo loved his son.

"I won't have to kill you," Gabriel continued. "I won't have to shed first blood. Your faggot son doesn't count. But watching him die will break you. Everyone will know you're not fit to control our family."

Every fiber of my being rebelled at his words. Joseph wasn't going to die. I couldn't let him die.

I twisted in his hold, ignoring the pain as some of my hair was ripped out of my scalp. I managed to drive my elbow into his doughy stomach. The air whooshed out of his lungs, and his grip on me eased as he doubled over, wheezing.

I ran toward Joseph, throwing myself at Ricky

with a defiant shriek. His eyes widened, and he was too surprised to react in time.

I didn't know how to fight, but I did know how to hurt a man. I slammed into him with enough momentum to shove him and his gun away from Joseph. Then, I rammed my knee up into his balls.

He dropped to his knees, clutching at his crotch and gasping for air.

"Joseph," I sobbed, struggling to get my shoulders under his arm to help him to his feet.

He got one foot down to support himself, but his boot slipped in a pool of his blood, and he went back down.

"Stupid bitch." Gabriel's fingers dug into my upper arm, and I shrieked as he wrenched me away from Joseph.

He spun my body away from his and threw me onto the table. My head cracked against the wood, making my skull throb and my stomach turn. His hand pressed between my shoulders, pinning me down hard enough that my breasts ached against the unyielding table.

I heard the sound of a belt buckle being loosened, a zipper being lowered.

Joseph snarled, and I felt something hard pressing against my ass.

"Your son can watch me fuck his whore while he bleeds out," Gabriel told Mr. Russo.

I screamed and slapped my sweaty palms against the polished wood, struggling to get free. But Gabriel had me trapped, his hand pinning me in place while his hips trapped mine against the edge of the table.

A shot rang out, and I screamed again, fearing for Joseph.

A heavy weight fell onto my back, driving the air from my lungs.

Two more shots, in quick succession.

"Ashlyn!"

"Marco," I sobbed his name.

The weight was lifted from my back, and I realized Gabriel's dead body had fallen onto me. I watched Marco heave his lifeless form aside before he reached for me, running his hands over my body to check for injuries.

The man who had held a gun on Mr. Russo was on the floor, moaning and clutching his shoulder. Marco's father stood over him, his head cocked to one side. His black eyes betrayed no emotion when he emptied another round into the man's skull. He looked up at Mr. Russo and nodded, as though everything was handled.

"Joseph," I gasped, trying to move past Marco to get to him.

Joseph lay on his side, blood pooling around him. At first, I thought it was all Joseph's blood. But then I saw Ricky's ruined face, and I realized a lot of it was flowing from the hole in his skull.

I gagged, but I focused my attention back on Joseph. I struggled past Marco, stumbling to my knees beside Joseph. He wasn't moving, and his eyes were closed. But I could see his chest rising and falling.

He's not dead. He's not going to die.

I heard Mr. Russo shouting into his phone for an ambulance, saying something about a robbery. I wasn't sure how he planned to cover up three murders, but I didn't care. All I cared about was getting Joseph to the hospital.

Marco joined me, his face drawn with fear as he reached for Joseph's hand. I took Joseph's other hand in mine. I squeezed his fingers, willing him to squeeze mine back.

He didn't stir.

I choked on a sob, and I leaned into Marco's chest for support.

He can't die. I couldn't lose Joseph, or I'd lose half my heart.

Chapter Fourteen
JOSEPH

My recent memories were fuzzy. I'd drifted in and out for... How long?

I wasn't sure. All I knew was there were moments of pain, and then a warm fog would take it away.

Someone's hand covered mine. But it wasn't the small, soft hand I craved.

Ashlyn.

The last thing I could remember clearly was her pained expression as Gabriel Costa ripped her away from me.

My eyes snapped open, and I jolted forward. An erratic beeping sounded around me, but I ignored it, as well as the pain that knifed through my lower back.

"Easy, son." Dad's hand left mine to touch my

shoulder, guiding me back down onto the hospital bed.

"Ashlyn," I ground out her name as I gritted my teeth against the pain. I had to get to her. I had to know she was safe.

"Ashlyn is fine. She's with Marco." My father's lips twisted around the last statement.

"Costa," I growled his name, remembering the way he and his men had hurt her. "Where is he?"

"He's dead. Leo killed him." He didn't even blink when he told me Marco's dad had killed his rival. "That little shit Matt ran straight to Gabriel after he saw... Well, after he saw you. Marco and Leo tracked him down and found out that Gabriel had come for me at the restaurant. They got to us in time to save you.

"Leo's in lockup at the moment," Dad added. "We couldn't fully explain everything away as a robbery gone wrong, but he'll post bail and be out in no time."

I nodded, not really caring about Marco's father. He always managed to get out of serving jail time. I was sure he'd manage it again.

"What about you?" I asked. "Have the cops been hassling you?" I might not like my father's criminal lifestyle, but I didn't want him to go to jail.

"I'll be fine. Don't worry about me, son. Just focus on getting better."

But I couldn't focus on that. I couldn't focus on anything but Ashlyn. I wouldn't be able to rest until I saw she was safe.

"Where are Ashlyn and Marco?"

Dad sighed, his expression drooping with disappointment. "I told them they couldn't see you yet. I wanted to talk to you." His pale eyes glinted, his jaw firming with anger. "And they're not your family."

"They are," I countered. "I know you don't understand, but they are my family, Dad."

"No, I don't understand. But I don't want to see my only son murdered because he's... Because of his unorthodox choices." I knew he was swallowing a dirtier word, and I appreciated his tact.

"Once you're better, you're going to have to leave New York," he continued. "All of you. Ashlyn doesn't belong here, and Marco's not welcome here anymore, either."

I knew my father would think of my exile as a punishment, but he had no idea the gift he'd just given me: a way out.

"Thanks, Dad," I said earnestly. "Are we alright? I mean, I know you're not happy about all this, but we're still on speaking terms, right?"

His eyes sparkled with a glimmer of tears. "I thought I was going to lose you. I thought you were going to bleed out on the floor while I watched.

Maybe if that hadn't happened, I'd throw you out and never speak to you again. As it is..." He swiped at the wetness on his face. "Call me anytime, son. If you ever need anything, just call me."

"I will," I promised. "What about Mom? How is she taking all this?"

He waved his hand dismissively. "Your mother is furious at Ashlyn for stealing you away. Give her some time, and she'll cool off. She loves you too."

"Can I see her? Ashlyn, I mean. I want to see her and Marco."

Dad's lips thinned when I mentioned Marco's name, but he nodded. "I'll go tell them they can come in."

"Thanks, Dad," I said, more grateful for his loving nature than ever. My father might be a ruthless criminal, but he loved me and cared about my happiness.

Dad slipped out the door, and a minute later, Ashlyn burst into the room. She held a handful of colorful get-well-soon balloons, and she pulled Marco along in her wake. From the bemused expression on his face, he was happy to be pulled wherever she wanted him to go.

Ashlyn rushed to my side and released the balloons in her haste to grab my hand. Marco caught them before they could float away and knotted the ribbons to the guardrail on my hospital bed.

"Joseph," she said my name on a relieved sigh. She looked like she wanted to fling herself on top of me, but she stopped herself, settling for holding my hand. "I was so worried about you." Tears spilled from her lovely sapphire eyes.

I reached up and wiped them away. "I'm okay, angel."

I caught her chin between my thumb and forefinger, turning her face so I could inspect her. One of the last things I could remember was Ricky hitting her with his gun.

I locked eyes with Marco, knowing he'd give me an honest answer. "How is she?"

Physically, she looked fine, but my memories were hazy, and I couldn't recall everything that'd happened after I got stabbed.

Marco wrapped his arm around her waist and pulled her close. "Our girl's a fighter. She's okay."

"Yes, I'm fine," she insisted. "But you need to rest," she told me firmly. "I'm going to call the nurse to get you more pain meds."

"Don't," I insisted. "I want to talk to you. Both of you."

Marco hit the call button for the nurse. "Talk fast. Then, rest."

I glared at him for being so high-handed, but I

didn't waste time arguing. "We're leaving New York," I told them. "Dad says we have to."

Marco's eyes lit up with hope. "What?"

"We're out, Marco. We can leave. They don't want us here anymore."

"Really?" Ashlyn gasped, her tears falling faster. "It's over? We can all go back to Cambridge now?"

"Is that where you want to go?" I asked her. "You don't have to go back to Harvard if you don't want to."

"I'd love to go back. I want to finish school. On my terms."

I squeezed her hand. "Then that's what we'll do, angel."

The nurse appeared, ready to administer more pain meds. I thought about refusing, but one hard look from Marco silenced me.

"We'll be right here when you wake up," he promised.

Ashlyn brushed a kiss over my cheek. "Get some rest. I love you, Joseph."

Her words of love followed me down as I sank back into sleep.

Chapter Fifteen
MARCO

Four Months Later

Ashlyn whined and wiggled in Joseph's ropes. Her arms were drawn tight behind her, bound from shoulders to wrists. A blindfold covered her lovely eyes, and he'd just introduced her to a wicked new toy: nipple clamps.

She was on her knees in the middle of the bed, and he loomed behind her, stroking her skin in a teasing caress that drove her wild.

I increased my pace, my hand flying over the page as my light pencil strokes captured the beauty before me. I used to draw from memory, but now that I was taking my art more seriously, I wanted a live model. Ashlyn was the perfect woman for the job.

When I could pry her away from her studies and urge Joseph away from his classes at Boston University, they helped me create my sensual drawings. I was developing something of an online following, and I was able to sell my work. I'd even started earning enough to cover our bills for the townhouse we'd bought in the South End. Dad had given me a chunk of cash and a "good riddance" on my way out of New York, but being with my new family—Joseph and Ashlyn—eased the sting of abandonment. And being able to help support us financially gave me a sense of personal pride I'd never known before.

Ashlyn let out the sexiest little whimper, and I couldn't hold back any longer. I set my drawing aside and snapped a picture on my phone for later reference. My balls ached and my dick throbbed, desperate to get inside her. I couldn't sit back and sketch for even a second more.

I had to fuck her, had to touch her. I was as addicted to her as ever, and so was Joseph. Our pretty, clever little princess. She was focusing on her academics, but I knew that ultimately, her dream was to have a family. With both of us. We didn't bother to hide our unconventional relationship now that we were free of our families' expectations. We made our own choices and lived to make each other happy. No one else mattered.

Joseph noticed that I'd set my work aside. He shot me a wicked grin and removed the clamps from Ashlyn's nipples. She shrieked and writhed as blood rushed back to the abused buds. Joseph petted her wet pussy, making her cry morph into a desperate little whine.

I closed the distance between us and removed her blindfold. She stared up at me, her shining eyes dark with erotic pain. She'd taken to Joseph's games beautifully, but I'd always be here to take care of her when he was a little harsh with her.

I cupped her jaw and traced the line of her lower lip with my thumb.

"Poor little princess," I cooed. "Did Joseph hurt your pretty nipples?"

"Yes, Daddy," she whispered, tipping her head back as Joseph continued to stroke her swollen labia.

"I'll kiss it better," I promised, dropping to my knees by the edge of the bed. I captured one of the abused buds between my lips, gently rubbing away the discomfort with my tongue.

She groaned and thrust her chest toward my mouth, welcoming more. I moved my attention to her other nipple, soothing it as well. After a minute, she began to moan and rock her hips against Joseph's hand, seeking more stimulation.

"I think our girl needs to be fucked," I told Joseph.

"I think so too," he agreed, his voice deep with his own, darker lust. "She's earned it."

"Yes," she begged. "Please, Sir. Please, Daddy."

My cock jerked toward her, and Joseph's jaw clenched with his own need. He was already naked, and I quickly undressed so I could join them.

Joseph lay down on his back, and I shifted Ashlyn so that she straddled his hips, facing away from him. He scooted her to the edge of the bed, and when I stood, her lips lined up with my dick.

"Lower yourself onto Joseph's cock." She'd been such a good girl, waiting for my command.

His fingers curved into her hips, controlling her pace as he slowly guided her down onto his length. Once he was fully inside her, I brushed my cockhead against her lips, letting her taste my pre-cum.

She knew better than to try to suck me off right away. While Joseph gripped her hips and guided her to ride his cock, she started to kiss my dick, licking me and pressing her lips against me. I stared down at her, intoxicated by her reverence for me, by her complete devotion. Ashlyn didn't hold anything back; she eagerly gave herself to both Joseph and me.

Despite the dirty things we did to her, she was just as pure and perfect as she'd been when we'd first met her.

"Open up, babygirl," I ordered, no longer able to stand her soft kisses. I needed the wet heat of her sweet mouth around me.

Her lips parted, and she welcomed me in as I slid all the way back to her throat. My girl had always been good a sucking cock, but in the last few months, I'd taught her exactly how Daddy liked it.

With her arms bound behind her, she needed me to help her balance. I wrapped her silky hair around my fist and braced her shoulder with my other hand, urging her to take me in slow, deep strokes.

Joseph increased his pace, and I heard him growl his need. He was close, but he'd make sure she came first. Her pleasure was always our first priority. She was devoted to us, and it was our responsibility to ensure her blissful happiness.

He eased his hold on her hips so she could control the pace, and he dipped one hand down to touch her clit. She whimpered around my cock, and I cursed as the sound tormented me with a surge of lust.

"Ride my cock," Joseph commanded. "Make yourself come, angel."

She started to grind against him, rotating her hips. I watched her small body tense as her pleasure crested. Joseph pinched her clit, and she screamed around my cock as her orgasm claimed her. Joseph groaned, his head dropping back as he thrust his hips up into her, riding out his own bliss.

I couldn't hold back. Now that my girl had been satisfied, I let go. I pressed deep into her throat and released my cum into her. She swallowed it all down, greedy for me. Her open hunger for both of us increased my pleasure, making me lightheaded with ecstasy.

I pulled free from her mouth and collapsed onto the bed. Joseph guided her off his cock and laid her between us, so we could both cuddle her close and stroke her. He left for a few seconds to retrieve his shears, and he cut away the ropes that bound her arms.

She let out a happy little sigh and closed her eyes, snuggling into my chest as Joseph rubbed her shoulders.

We both murmured words of love and praise as she softened between us, perfectly trusting and completely content.

Ashlyn was ours, and we'd never take her devotion for granted. We'd cherish her and protect her for the rest of our lives.

"I love you, Joseph," she murmured. "I love you, Daddy."

The words reached deep inside me, warming my chest and stoking my lust. My cock began to stiffen again, even though I'd just come inside her mouth.

She gasped when my dick pressed into her hip.

"Already?"

"Always for you, babygirl," I promised.

"Anything for you, angel," Joseph swore.

We held her between us and showed her just how much we worshipped her.

Chapter Sixteen
MARCO

The sunlight shined on Ashlyn's glossy hair, illuminating the lighter hues amongst the dark, silky locks. Delicate strands of auburn and spun gold shimmered over rich mahogany, and my rough, calloused fingertips itched to caress their silken length. Even from a distance, I caught the brilliant flash of her perfect smile as she laughed aloud at something her best friend, Jayme, had said.

I propped my shoulder against the building I'd been loitering beside while waiting for her to get out of class, enjoying the warmth of the bricks. The early April breeze was crisp enough that sheltering by the wall provided a comfortable place to wait while I indulged my obsession with her. I was perfectly content to observe her laughing with Jayme; I didn't want to cut her time with her friend short. Ashlyn was expecting me to meet her now that her classes were finished for the day, so it wasn't as though I was stalking her without her knowledge.

Although, if she'd tried to put up a fuss about me escorting her to and from campus, I wouldn't have hesitated to stalk her and make sure she was safe using the public transit between our house and her lecture hall.

But my good girl never put up a fuss when it came to serious matters like her safety. She liked that I wanted to take care of her, and I'd never felt more at peace than I did guarding her. I might be earning money selling my art, but protecting Ashlyn was my full-time job now. Ensuring her blissful happiness was my top priority, and that essential role brought me more contentment than I'd ever thought possible.

Even the bulky clothes that swaddled her mouth-watering figure couldn't diminish my keen attraction to her. My princess's lush curves were almost completely concealed beneath five layers of clothing. I imagined peeling off each knit, wooly barrier that separated my hands from her hot little body, until her bare skin pebbled from desire rather than the chilly weather.

The corners of my lips twitched, and my indulgent smile twisted with carnal hunger. I watched her with predatory focus, not feeling even a twinge of guilt over my possessive behavior when it came to Ashlyn. I loved when she looked up at me with those wide, innocent blue eyes, but in the last several months, I'd found a different sort of enjoyment in watching her from a distance, observing her interacting with her friends.

It still seemed surreal that we were here—Joseph and me living in Boston with our sweet girl. By some miracle, we'd been able to keep her for ourselves while also returning her to her normal life as a college student.

My chest swelled with pride. I'd never known satisfaction like the fulfilment I found in providing for my family: Ashlyn and Joseph. I'd left my only blood relative behind when my father had exiled me from New York with a curse on my name, but my chosen family embraced me in a way my father never had.

As though brought on by the fleeting thought of my old life, something ugly stirred in my gut. My body reacted to the threat a few heartbeats before my mind processed what the twist in my stomach meant. This wasn't an emotional response to thinking about my father; I hadn't experienced this base, aggressive reflex in months, and its sudden return shocked me like a sucker punch.

All my muscles coiled tight, preparing to attack. My senses sharpened, and the crisp air that had felt so pleasant beside the warm bricks now made my skin prickle with awareness. Although she was still too far away from me—halfway across Harvard Yard—Ashlyn's melodic laugh rang in my ears: alarm bells rather than the sweetest music.

Because I wasn't the only one watching her. A man trailed after her, keeping a calculated distance between them. His gaze locked on her back, tracking her movements. With his Harvard sweatshirt and stubble-free cheeks, he was young enough that I might have mistaken him for another student, mooning over my beautiful girl. But he hadn't exited the lecture hall along with her other classmates, and his stare was too intent to be simple admiration.

My feet were closing the distance between us before I could think. My fingers flexed, preparing to close around his neck and make sure he could never breathe the same air as her ever again.

"Marco!" Ashlyn called my name in a jubilant exhalation. Before I could get past her to reach the bastard, her slight body barreled into mine for our customary, enthusiastic hug.

I grasped her tightly to my chest and spun, putting my bulk between her and the man following her. Instinct urged me to release her immediately and remove the threat. But her soft, floral scent ensnared my focus, helping mitigate the brutal impulse enough that I was able to think like a rational man.

I can't kill a boy in broad daylight. Not on her college campus.

Not at all, I added the harsh internal addendum, my arms drawing her impossibly closer. That violent part of my life was over, the dark deeds firmly in my past. I would always protect Ashlyn, but I had to be better for her. She would never see me with blood on my hands. *Never.*

"Are you okay?" she asked, twining her arms around my shoulders to return my fierce hug, offering me support.

Fuck. I never wanted her to be scared again, and she would definitely be frightened if I told her someone was following her.

But I couldn't let the fucker slip away. Not without at least questioning him. No one from our former life should've followed us here. Maybe the guy was just some creep who was into Ashlyn.

Too bad for him, I wouldn't tolerate that shit, either.

I took a deep breath, inhaling her sweet scent to ground myself. There were other ways to handle this that didn't involve making a scene on campus. Ways that didn't involve scaring Ashlyn.

"I'm just happy to see you, babygirl," I hedged, brushing a kiss over her hair before releasing her from my too-tight embrace. I tucked a stray, silky lock behind her ear, and she leaned into my touch. Her sapphire eyes were so wide and trusting that my heart throbbed with a painful beat. My princess fully believed that I would take care of her. She felt completely safe with me, and I never wanted that to change.

"I'm taking you to the café." I trailed my thumb over her cheek, which was slightly chilled from the crisp breeze. "You need a pumpkin spice latte and a cinnamon scone."

She giggled, and the sound of her lighthearted joy rippled through my body in a warm, soothing wave. "How did you know?"

"It's my job to know." I pressed a quick kiss against her forehead before easing back. I shifted so that she was tucked by my side, my arm bracing her as close to my protective bulk as possible. With my free hand, I plucked the laptop bag from her shoulder and slung it onto mine.

"You don't have to carry that," she protested, eyeing the decidedly feminine, gold floral pattern embossed on the white leather.

"Yes, I do. That's my job, too." I rubbed my hand up and down her arm, warming her through her thick layers of clothing. "Come on, princess. Let's get you that hot latte."

I would get Ashlyn safely into the café, and then Joseph could protect her while I checked up on her stalker. The prickle on the back of my neck told me that the fucker was still nearby, watching us.

I was dimly aware of her sing-song goodbye to Jayme, and I managed a polite nod before whisking her away. As I ushered her off-campus, I tapped out a text to Joseph.

Date with our girl. Silver Spoon Café. Now.

As far as my best friend was concerned, he was about to join us on a spontaneous date; no need to upset him with the reality of the situation. He'd been so happy since we moved to Boston and left our violent lifestyle behind. I could handle this stalker on my own. I just needed Joseph to watch over our girl while I took care of the threat.

I could protect both of them. I could do all the dark, evil things necessary to keep them safe. As long as my family was happy, I could endure anything for them.

Thank you for reading THE DADDY AND THE DOM!

Joseph, Ashlyn, and Marco's story continues in THEIRS TO PROTECT.

THEIRS TO PROTECT EXCERPT

Marco

It took every ounce of my very limited restraint to stop myself from killing the creep who was stalking my sweet girl. I felt his eyes on us like an itch beneath my skin, a prickling awareness of a threat that'd become instinctive during the dark, ugly years I'd spent in the mafia. I thought I'd left these survival instincts behind when I'd been exiled from New York. Ashlyn was supposed to be safe here, returned to her normal world at Harvard.

I rubbed the back of my neck, attempting to scrub away the maddening sensation of the man's sinister focus. I couldn't confront the bastard until Joseph arrived. My best friend would watch over Ashlyn while I dealt with the threat.

For now, I couldn't so much as glare at the guy, even though he'd seated himself only three tables to our left in the bustling café. He'd folded his lanky body into a cozy armchair tucked in the far corner, masking his attention on Ashlyn by idly flipping through the pages of a heavy textbook.

But I'd noticed him watching her ever since she'd left her lecture hall twenty minutes ago, where I'd been waiting outside to escort her home from class. The fresh white lettering on his Harvard sweatshirt was too bright, and the Red Sox baseball cap pulled low over his heavy brows was too crisp. The clothes were brand new; this wasn't scruffy apparel that might be pulled on by a guy who'd snagged the first semi-clean items he'd found while rushing to class.

I'd tested him to ensure my instincts weren't pure paranoia. Rather than taking Ashlyn home, I'd suggested a spontaneous date at her favorite café on the outskirts of campus. While she'd texted Joseph with the invite to join us, I'd clocked her stalker changing course to follow us to our new destination.

Now, he sat only a few yards away from her, and the mounting impulse to kick his teeth in drew my muscles taut. It would take mere seconds to close the distance between us and haul his ass outside. I wouldn't risk Ashlyn getting caught up in a brawl. It would be so easy to separate him from her, to crush his bones beneath my fists until he confessed why he was stalking my babygirl. Until he begged for mercy and swore he'd never again attempt to so much as breathe the same air as her.

I rolled the mounting tension from my shoulders and forced my clenched fists to unfurl.

Not yet, I reasoned. *Not until Joseph gets here.*

He could shield Ashlyn from what I had to do. Neither of them needed to know about this threat. About the brutal way I'd handle it. Handle *him*.

If the creep knew what vicious scenes were playing through my mind, he'd get the fuck out of this café and never come near my princess ever again. But I needed to question him before I eliminated him as a threat. If anyone from our old life had followed us to Boston...

I tried to swallow down a growl, but a low grunt caught in my throat.

"Are you okay?" Ashlyn's soft concern ensnared my attention, her voice a soothing balm that calmed the itch to punish her stalker.

Her sapphire eyes peered up at me, and her lush lips pursed with worry. Long, slender fingers brushed over her laptop, moving to close it so she could turn her full focus on me.

I caught her dainty hand in mine, redirecting it to rest on the small table that separated us. "I'm fine, princess." I took a breath and smoothed the gruff edge from my tone. "Keep working on your paper."

A small furrow appeared between her delicately arched brows, and she glanced down at the open book in front of me. "Are you bored? You don't have to read my coursebooks if you don't enjoy them. Your art is already amazing."

I smoothed my free hand over the slightly glossy page without looking at it, keeping my gaze locked on her. I'd been staring at the images of Edgar Degas' nineteenth-century nude drawings for at least five minutes already, not really seeing them. My mind had been fixed on detailed scenes of how I'd punish the man who dared to watch my sweet girl, even though I'd managed to keep my narrowed eyes glued to the drawings instead of glaring at him. I couldn't risk spooking him before Joseph arrived.

"I know I don't have to. I want to." My tone came out deep and steady. The concern in her wide blue eyes soothed the beast in me, releasing my mind from its dark claws. Nothing mattered more than her safety and contentment. I wouldn't allow my protective fury to rattle her. I didn't want her to experience even one more second of the fear that she'd already endured while under threat from my former *family* in New York.

A wry smile twisted my mouth as my focus shifted

to her. The expression took little effort to fabricate, and after a few more heartbeats of staring into her lovely, trusting eyes, my full attention fixed on her needs rather than on my darkest urges to hurt her stalker.

My thick fingers were gentle as I traced soothing circles over her palm. "I like that you share your books with me. What kind of hack artist would I be if I ignored the expertise of a Harvard-educated art historian?"

Her alabaster skin flushed my favorite shade of pink, and the tension eased from her soft features. She wrapped her much smaller fingers around my hand, squeezing lightly. "Have I told you you're the best study buddy?"

The corners of my mouth twitched, the tugging sensation of a genuine, easy smile still somewhat strange to me. I'd never smiled so much in my life as I did now that Ashlyn was mine. "Only twice so far today."

Her brilliant grin hit me square in the chest. For a moment, I couldn't remember how to breathe, much less think about her stalker.

"Hmmm," she mused, her gemstone eyes sparkling as she lowered her voice to a conspiratorial whisper. "Twice isn't nearly enough. You're the best study buddy, Daddy."

My hand tightened around hers, and a low, hungry growl slipped between my teeth before I could contain the feral sound. "Are you teasing me, babygirl?"

An impertinent dimple shadowed her cheek. "Maybe."

"Definitely," I rumbled. "If you want a spanking, you can always ask me nicely, princess."

Her face flushed scarlet, and her wide eyes darted around the café to check if anyone had overheard. She shushed me dramatically, and I chuckled.

"That cute little blush will attract a lot more attention," I informed her with a taunting smile. "Are you sorry for teasing Daddy?"

"Marco!" she hissed, squirming in her seat.

I hummed my satisfaction. I would definitely enjoy turning her over my knee as soon as we got home. I wanted her pert ass to match the enticing shade of red that colored her cheeks. Already, my palm tingled with the remembered warmth of her enflamed skin. It'd been too long since the last time I'd properly taken her in hand. My good girl was rarely naughty, but she clearly needed to feel my discipline. I knew she'd been more stressed than usual with her studies, so I'd eased back from the stricter physical aspects of our dynamic to give her time to focus on her academics.

That had been a mistake. She needed release from all that responsibility, and I hadn't been fulfilling my role. Suddenly, I could hardly wait to get to the privacy of our own home so I could give her exactly what she needed.

"Is Marco tormenting you, angel?" Joseph appeared at her side and leaned in to brush a kiss over her red cheek. I'd been so entranced by her that I hadn't even noticed his approach.

His lips hovered at her ear, teasing her sensitive skin as he murmured, "Tormenting you is *my* job. You must have done something very naughty to provoke Marco. I guess I'll have to punish you, too."

She squeezed her eyes shut, but a small smile still curved her lips. "Oh my god!" she squeaked. "We're in *public*."

"You started this little game, princess," I reminded her evenly. "You knew exactly what you were getting into. Pack up your things. We're taking you home."

She drew in a little panting breath and licked her lips, equal parts anxious and aroused. "But Joseph just got here. He hasn't even ordered his coffee. We were supposed to have a date." She made a pretty pout in my direction, goading me further.

My hand firmed around hers, and I leaned in slowly, imposing the weight of my censure. She tried to ease back, but Joseph wrapped his arm around her shoulders and locked her in place. A wicked grin illuminated his model-handsome features when she trembled against him.

"Are you going to pack up, or is Joseph going to have to do it for you?" I enunciated each word in a slow, heavy cadence.

Her mouth twisted in an impish smirk. "How can I pack up when you're holding my hand so tightly?"

Joseph's low laugh rolled over my dark chuckle, and she shivered.

"Wrong answer, angel." He pressed a doting kiss to her temple and started loading her laptop and books into her bag.

"Was it?" Her saucy challenge hitched slightly, but our girl continued to willfully provoke me.

Joseph groaned softly, and I knew her teasing was tempting him just as keenly as it was tormenting me. "You'll have to go crying to Marco when you can't sit comfortably tomorrow," he warned.

"Tomorrow?" I rasped. "Make that next week."

Her lush lips popped open, my threat finally shocking that mischievous little smile off her lovely face.

"Don't worry, babygirl." I brushed her knuckles with my thumb. "I know what you need. I'll take good care of you."

"We both will," Joseph promised, grasping her other hand in his.

He passed me her laptop bag, and I slung it over my shoulder, not giving a fuck that the white leather was embossed with shiny, gold flowers that were decidedly feminine. I loved buying pretty things for Ashlyn, and I was proud to bear the weight of her books to spare her from the strain.

I'd been so captivated by her delectable blush and shy smile that I'd completely forgotten about her stalker for a few perfect, sweet minutes. But as soon as we walked within peripheral sight of the corner where the man had settled in with a latte and a book, his keen attention scraped over my skin. The raw sensation on my nerve endings snapped me back to acute awareness of the threat he posed.

Joseph didn't seem to notice. He was totally lost in his obsession with Ashlyn, and he'd always been a better man than me. His good heart had allowed him to easily adapt to our new life, as though he'd always belonged here. I was a suspicious, mean bastard, and I'd never fully lose the darkness embedded in my soul.

It was better this way, really. Joseph could remain with Ashlyn, keeping her content while I shielded them both from the harsher realities of the world. Those harsh realities had been horrible enough to make Joseph abandon me once, when he'd fled to Cambridge in the first place and met Ashlyn in her safe little bubble. I wouldn't risk losing him again by making him aware that we might not be free of our violent lives, after all.

I wouldn't lose either of them. I would keep and protect my family, no matter what it took.

Joseph, Ashlyn, and Marco's story continues in THEIRS TO PROTECT.

ALSO BY JULIA SYKES

Mafia Ménage Trilogy

Mafia Captive

The Daddy and The Dom

Theirs to Protect

The Captive Series

Sweet Captivity

Claiming My Sweet Captive

Stealing Beauty

Captive Ever After

Pretty Hostage

Wicked King

Ruthless Savior

The Impossible Series

Impossible

Savior

Rogue

Knight

Mentor

Master

King

A Decadent Christmas (An Impossible Series Christmas Special)

Czar

Crusader

Prey (An Impossible Series Short Story)

Highlander

Decadent Knights (An Impossible Series Short Story)

Centurion

Dex

Hero

Wedding Knight (An Impossible Series Short Story)

Valentines at Dusk (An Impossible Series Short Story)

Nice & Naughty (An Impossible Series Christmas Special)

Dark Lessons

RENEGADE

The Dark Grove Plantation Series

Holden

Brandon

Damien

Printed in Great Britain
by Amazon